FLASHPOINT

Also by Leo Kessler:

THE IRON FIST
THE TRAITORS
WOLF
BREAKTHROUGH

In the *Wotan/Panzer* Series:
SS PANZER BATTALION
DEATH'S HEAD
CLAWS OF STEEL
GUNS AT CASSION
THE DEVIL'S SHIELD
HAMMER OF THE GODS
FORCED MARCH
BLOOD AND ICE
THE SAND PANTHERS
COUNTER-ATTACK
PANZER HUNT
SLAUGHTER GROUND

In the *Black Cossacks* Series:
THE BLACK COSSACKS
THE BLACK COSSACKS 2: SABRES OF THE REICH
THE BLACK COSSACKS 3: MOUNTAIN OF SKULLS

In the *Stormtroop* Series:
STORMTROOP
BLOOD MOUNTAIN
VALLEY OF THE ASSASSINS
RED ASSAULT

In the *Rommel* Series:
GHOST DIVISION
MASSACRE

In the *Foreign Legion* Series:
HELLFIRE

Leo Kessler

Flashpoint

Macdonald Futura Publishers Ltd

A Futura Book

First published in Great Britain by
Macdonald Futura Publishers Ltd in 1980

ISBN 0 7088 1926 5
Printed and bound in Great Britain by
©ollins, Glasgow

Macdonald Futura Publishers Ltd
Paulton House, 8 Shepherdess Walk
London N1 7LW

One
Flipper Flosse

ONE

'Heil Hitler!'

The voice was firm and incisive, yet somehow a little cynical. No one moved. Someone farted weakly.

At the door, his tunic powdered with the snow which was still falling outside, the young, one-armed officer stared around at the miserable, unshaven collection of soldiers which the freezing Eifel schoolhouse contained, his gaze full of both cynicism and compassion, as if he had seen this all before and would probably see it again before the long war was over.

These were the survivors, what was left of the Reich's finest divisions, decimated the month before in the snow-bound Ardennes. They were all represented: the *Adolf Hitler Bodyguard*, its giants now frail, shaken wrecks; the *Hitler Youth*, the ruthless look gone now from the youthful faces of those teenage fanatics, the *Reich*, the *17th Panzer Grenadiers*, the pathetic handful of men left from *SS Assault Regiment Wotan*, which had suffered the most casualties of all those proud, confident SS formations which had rolled into the Ardennes battle in December 1944.

The young, one-armed officer shook his head a little sadly, and told himself that there didn't seem much he could do with a bunch like this. With his good foot he kicked the door closed behind him and deadened the low rumble of the permanent artillery barrage in the hills beyond the Eifel village. 'Not a pretty sight, I must confess,' he said with forced cheerfulness. 'Not a very pretty sight at all.' With the fingers of his one hand, he deftly removed the silver top of his black malacca cane and raised the stock to his lips.

Crouched in a corner with a grey Army blanket wrapped around his shoulders, Sergeant-Major Schulze, Wotan's senior surviving NCO, watched enviously as the young officer swallowed the drink which the cane obviously contained, licking his parched cracked lips as he did so. At his side, Matz, blue and trembling violently with the freezing cold like a leaf in the wind, croaked: 'God, I'd almost let 'em dock a loop of my dick for a slug of that sauce!'

'What do you make of him, ape-turd?' Schulze asked by way of a reply, his eyes still on that upraised cane.

'He's an officer,' Matz said, as if the word explained everything.

'I know that, arse with ears,' Schulze said impatiently. 'But look at him, one flipper gone, a pegleg too if I'm not mistaken, and not one single piece of tin on his chest. So where's he bin for the last five years, eh?' Schulze's red-rimmed eyes took in the young officer's white face, which looked as if it had not been exposed to fresh air for a long while, and the lighter patches on his tunic where once there might have been many decorations, the 'tin', about which he had just spoken.

'Punishment battalion perhaps, Schulze.' Matz shrugged carelessly. 'Why ask me – I'm not Jesus, yer know?'

The young officer screwed the silver cap back on as deftly as he had removed it and beamed at the shivering men squatting on the straw-covered floor of the schoolroom. 'Gentlemen, I hate to disturb your undoubtedly well-earned siesta in this charming country retreat you have found yourselves here, but I need bodies – volunteers.' There was a subdued groan from his listeners and again someone gave a contemptuous fart.

The young officer continued to beam down at them. 'I'm completely overwhelmed by such enthusiasm, gentlemen,' he said cheerfully. 'But perhaps I should first introduce myself. Under-Lieutenant Flosse[1].' With his black cane he tapped the empty sleeve tucked neatly into his belt. '*Nomen est omen*, as you scholars of Greek with have undoubtedly already remarked. Flosse is now minus one of his fins. Hence the name I enjoyed with my own beloved troops in the past – "One-Flipper Flosse".'

[1] The German word for 'fin'.

Schulze grunted his approval. The officer wasn't the usual SS fire-eater out for glory, 'tin' – and early death for Folk, Fatherland and Führer. He'd been around. One-Flipper Flosse smiled at them cynically. 'I can see that my appeal to the spirit of self-sacrifice and patriotism has had little effect,' he remarked easily. 'Tut-tut, what *has* become of the Armed SS's celebrated elan?'

'Up my arse, Lieutenant!' someone growled from his listeners.

Politely, One-Flipper Flosse addressed himself to the bearded NCO of the *Reich*, his head wrapped in a blood-stained dirty bandage, who had spoken. 'You said something, Sergeant?'

'I said – "up my arse". The day before Christmas my company went into action at Bastogne. But those lousy Ami dive-bombers caught us out in the open. We came out, all our Tigers gone and all our officers. There was only me and a dozen other stubble-hoppers left.' The NCO spat contemptuously into the straw at his feet. 'And *you* want volunteers!'

'Yes, yes, it was the same with us,' angry voices agreed from all over the room, the men's breath congealing in little grey clouds on the freezing air.

'Oh, knock it off!' Schulze snarled. 'Yer don't want me to have me periods prematurely, do you?' He looked around at the survivors' faces angrily. 'You shower o' shit should have been at Kursk in forty-three, then you would have really had something to crap about!'

One-Flipper Flosse turned to Schulze, his eyes full of sudden interest. 'Ah, I see, Sergeant-Major, you are from the celebrated Wotan, commanded by the late – er – Colonel von Dodenburg. I've heard a great deal about your regiment.

Schulze said nothing.

Next to him Matz dropped his gaze to the floor. None of the Wotan's survivors wanted to be reminded of the fact that they had lost their beloved CO in the recent offensive.

'How many of you are there, Sergeant-Major?'

Schulze wiped his big paw of a hand across his cracked mouth. The officer understood immediately, but instead of unscrewing the silver cap, this time, he pressed a switch at the side of the cane. A trap opened to reveal a cigar, neatly wrapped in foil. 'Have a cigar, my dear Sergeant-Major,' he said and tendered it to a surprised Schulze.

The NCO took his time lighting it and after the first deep draw, which set him off coughing like some asthmatic in his death throes and which brought him envious looks from all sides, he said, 'We're two NCOs, me and this wooden-legged cripple next to me, and about fifty other ranks.'

'Officers?'

'We brought out half a dozen. But the bone-merchants have got hold of all of them over at Cologne.'

'Bad?' Schulze nodded, rubbing the white tip of his frost-bitten nose thoughtfully. He looked enquiringly at Matz.

The little corporal said nothing. He nodded at the cigar. Wordlessly Schulze handed it over. 'What do you need the bodies for, sir?' he asked after a moment. The cynical look vanished from the young officer's face. 'They'd have the knickers off me in Berlin if I told you that, Sergeant-Major. State secret, can't tell you that.'

'I see, sir.' Schulze said, savouring the word 'Berlin'. Finally he asked, 'What's in it for Mrs Schulze's handsome son – and the rest of Wotan?'

'You're a sly dog, Sergeant-Major.'

'It's a hard life for us common soldiers, sir. A man's got to look out for himself. Our kind's lucky to get a glass of beer now and – '

The officer stopped the old phrase with a wave of his cane. He considered for a few seconds, while Schulze watched him, noting the determined chin and the deep, well-set eyes. One-Flipper Flosse was an experienced leader of men all right, although that bare tunic revealed nothing of where he might have gained that experience. 'My orders are to report to the old Lichtenfelde Barracks of the *Bodyguard* immediately, with whatever volunteers I can find here . . .'

He paused momentarily. 'However, with the present state of the railways, the bombings and this terrible winter weather, who could say how long a trip from this arsehole of the world to Berlin might take?'

'Who indeed, sir?' Matz echoed expansively, taking another happy puff at the cigar.

'Hamburg, sir – *forty-eight hours?*' Schulze asked tentatively.

'Hamburg – *twenty-four hours?*' the officer countered.

'*Thirty-six?*' Schulze parried.

'All right, *thirty-six* it is.'

Schulze looked enquiringly at Matz. The latter's face lit up, the first time since they had commenced that terrible retreat from the Ardennes the previous month.[1]

'Pay in advance?' he queried.

'Pay in advance – and a kilo of free Parisians per man for all I care,' One-Flipper said happily.

'*Carambo-cracko, a whisky, a wine!*' Schulze exploded happily, launching a tremendous slap at Matz's skinny back and almost making him swallow the cigar. 'Did you hear that, you little pubic-hair louse? We're off to the Waterfront! A thirty-six-hour stopover in Hamburg!' He made a vulgar grab at the front of his tattered, grimy field-grey trousers. 'I've got so much ink in my pen, I don't even know who to write to!'

Matz recovered from his attempts not to swallow the cigar and said, 'When that pavement slit in the *Reeperbahn* knows old Matzi's coming, they'll start drawing their money out of the savings bank to pay *me*, cos they know that when Matzi snakes 'em, they stay snaked for a long time!' He nodded his head in self-congratulatory approval and poked a dirty thumb at his skinny chest. 'Women have been known to scream in fear when they've seen what I've got in my britches – *grown women!*'

Schulze contained his enthusiasm. 'When do you want us, sir?' he snapped, some of the old fire in his voice.

One-Flipper Flosse stared at Schulze's broad, honest face

[1] See L. Kessler: *The Hammer of the Gods.*

and then at those of the other Wotan men, like someone who might be trying to impress their features on his mind's eye in case he never saw those same faces again. 'Now,' he said finally.

'All right, you heroes,' Schulze bellowed so that the whole room echoed and the crucifix, its sole decoration, tumbled from the bare wall. 'You heard what the officer said, didn't you? Haul ass!'

Almost sadly, One-Flipper Flosse raised his malacca cane to his cap in salute and then he passed out into the driving snow, his shoulders suddenly hunched, as if in defeat . . .

TWO

Lichtenfelde Barracks, the pre-war home of the black-clad giants of the *Bodyguard*, was no longer the place it had once been. Most of the big barracks' upper storeys were shattered ruins and below everywhere, the bomb-damaged walls were shored up by timbers, with most of the windows long boarded-up. The giants, 'the asphalt soldiers' as they had once been called behind their backs in the SS because they seemed always to be parading through Berlin, had vanished too to be replaced by the grey-faced, creeping survivors of six years of war. Minus an eye, a leg, an arm, a hand, the 'base stallions' crept around the shattered barracks making an audible noise as they did so. As Matz contemptuously remarked to Schulze, watching the 'base stallions' perform their menial duties, 'I shouldn't be surprised, looking at that lot, if all the pavement pounders they've got around here haven't got artificial slits too.'

But the Wotan men wouldn't have time to find out if that awesome prediction were true or not; their stay in the former home of the *Bodyguard* was obviously going to be of limited duration.

On their first day there they were kept busy till nightfall.

Each man was issued with a new uniform, boots, the latest model Schmeisser machine pistol and, most surprisingly of all, one hundred captured English *Woodbine* cigarettes. As the ancient storeroom bulls started to hand out the fine English cigarettes, men clutched their chests and pretended to faint. Others rubbed their eyes as if wiping away tears, and one awed Wotan trooper remarked in a hushed voice, 'Heaven, arse and cloudburst, they'll expect us to march to Moscow – and back – for this kind of lung torpedo!'

Even Schulze, nursing a tremendous hangover from his thirty-hour drunk in his native Hamburg and harbouring the faint suspicion that the reason he was 'pissing five ways at once' (as he put it in his usual delicate manner to Matz) was because he'd caught a slight 'dose of the old blue-balls' on the *Reeperbahn*, was surprised – and suspicious.

That first morning he had heard a strange roaring sound coming from the far corner of the huge barracks and beyond the old stables he had seen a cloud of thick, oily-black smoke ascending to the grey January sky. That same afternoon, as he walked – a little painfully – to the bone merchants to have his aching parts washed out with the usual pink solution, he had caught a glimpse of a curious-looking object with two great rubber tyres. The thing was shaped like a blunt boat's prow and, in place of the bowsprit, there was a big steel pipe cased in what appeared to be armour-plating. He had been about to limp across to it and examine it more thoroughly, when he had felt a light tap on his shoulder. It was One-Flipper Flosse's malacca cane. Smiling evenly at the big NCO he had said, 'Curiosity killed the poor old roof-hare, you know. Better be off now and get those dreadful blue-balls of yours seen to. I'm sure that where we're going there'll be no VD merchants.' And he had waited until Schulze had saluted and limped off to the bone-merchants.

'What do you make of it, ape-turd?' Schulze asked Matz that night as they sat together over weak wartime beer in the NCO's canteen, idly watching a group of the cripples playing *skat* at another table.

Matz shrugged and took a drink of his beer. He pulled a wry face, as if he had just tasted something highly unpleasant. 'Search me, Schulze. All I know is that nothing good will come of it. New dice-beakers, real leather at that, and free Tommy cancer sticks.' He tugged at the end of his nose, reddened by years of cheap schnapps and the murderous Russian winters. 'My old hooter tells me that. That One-Flipper Flosse is preparing us for the chop, Schulze, that's old Matzi's guess.'

'You can say that again, pal,' one of the *skat* players growled from the other table. 'If anyone can land us poor stubble-hoppers with our hooters right down in the crap, it's the major.'

'Major?' Schulze queried.

'Yes, Flosse with the one flipper – *that* major,' the other man answered and rubbed the heavy stubble on his chin with a leather-gloved wooden hand. 'He got me this back in forty-two in the Crimea. A year later he got his, trying another of those damnfool stunts of his.' His face contorted scornfully. 'Fancy trying to fight off a T-34 with nothing better than a rifle-grenade! But you've got to give it to One-Flipper, he's a brave bastard if there ever was one.'

'Tell me more, pal,' Schulze said, leaning forward. 'Why's he back down to under-lieutenant? What's he done?'

'Don't you know?' the other man asked, surprised.

'No.'

'Christ on a crutch, I thought the whole of the Armed SS knew that! All of Berlin does.'

'We've happened to have been fighting a little war, pal,' Matz said pointedly. 'While you rear-echelon stallions have been broadening yer arses here in Berlin. Get on with it!'

But the two running-mates of Wotan were not fated to hear any more of One-Flipper Flosse's story that evening. Just as their informant opened his mouth again to tell them, presumably, why the officer had suffered such a surprising demotion, there was the tin wail of the air-raid sirens and the lights went out abruptly. 'The shitting Tommies again with their square eggs,' somebody grumbled, and then the canteen manager was bawling, 'All right, off'n yer keesters, you NCOs! Down into the cellars, everyone! You know what standing orders state . . .'

On the morning of Wotan's third day at the Berlin barracks, a fine day for January, with the sun a pale-gold ball in a crisp hard blue sky and the faint wind coming straight from Siberia, One-Flipper Flosse paraded them on the barracks square. After Schulze had reported his men all present and correct and had been ordered to stand them at ease, One-Flipper had walked up and down on the hard crisp snow in front of them, his eyes on the ground, as if he were debating something of importance with himself. Finally he stopped and spun round on them. 'Gentlemen, I can't tell you where we are going yet and what our mission is to be. But I can show you your weapons. They are not the best I must admit, but with most divisions these days reduced to a couple of battalions of armour, we must be thankful that *Reichsführer* Himmler saw his way to granting us these.'

Schulze shot a significant look at Matz at the mention of Himmler's name. Obviously they were on to something big. One-Flipper Flosse raised his officer's alert whistle to his lips and blew a shrill blast. The answering roar of tank motors was almost instantaneous. A second later, a squat heavy shape crawled around the corner and on to the square, spurting up a white wake of snow.

'Shit on shingle!' Matz gasped, recognizing the old-fashioned slow tank, 'a Frog Char B! We were knocking those off with pea-shooters back in 1940!'

One-Flipper nodded his agreement. 'Quite correct, Corporal. Your tank recognition ability is excellent.'

But there were more to come of the same vintage: a couple of light Czech Skoda chassis, with a German 75mm cannon mounted on them to make a primitive self-propelled gun; two battered Panzer Mark IIIs, with the gleaming holes where anti-tank shells had entered them years before clearly visible; a captured American Sherman armed with the lighter 57mm cannon instead of the new 75mm; and a motley collection of Italian, German and Russian armoured personnel carriers.

One-Flipper waited till the last Russian half-track had vanished on the other side of the barracks square before raising his voice and announcing in his cynical manner, 'Gentleman, you have just viewed Battle-Group Flosse.'

'Kiss me, Mother,' someone groaned in the ranks of the Wotan. 'You could crack that lot of old junk with a blunt tin-opener!'

'How right you are, soldier,' One-Flipper Flosse agreed. 'But let me show you my *pièce de résistance*. Perhaps it might heighten your faith in this new battle-group of mine.' Again Flosse raised his whistle. This time he blew two blasts upon it. There was an answering clatter of metal tracks. Next moment a battered English Churchill tank swung round the corner, towing behind it the strange object that Schulze had spotted that first afternoon at Lichtenfelde.

One-Flipper Flosse waited till the forty-ton Churchill and its trailer had come to a halt in front of Wotan, then he commanded: 'Break ranks and come view One-Flipper's ugly little toy.'

The men crowded around the long, squat, Tommy tank curiously. The officer rapped its metal side with his cane like a lecturer and said, 'The Tommies call it a Crocodile, and by our last count, according to Intelligence, there were exactly fifty of them in the whole of the Allied armies in Europe, no, as you were, forty-nine, now that one of our patrols – hm – *borrowed* this one from the Tommies in Holland last month.'

Schulze stared at the tank. He had seen Churchills enough at Dieppe in '42 and in Normandy the previous summer. There seemed nothing particular about this one, save for the trailer it towed. Then he noticed the ugly little nozzle with two metal tongues above it, like the points of a spark-plug, at the spot in the deck where normally the co-driver's machine gun would be mounted. At the same time he became aware too of the constant hissing and ticking from inside the trailer – like the hushing noise made by a locomotive waiting to draw a train out of a station. He frowned.

One-Flipper Flosse noticed the frown on the big Hamburger's face and said cheerfully, 'Do not frown, dear Sergeant-Major, for in one moment all will be explained. You see this particular monster is very special indeed. All of you are familiar with flame-throwers. The German Army has had them since the First World War. Some of you may have also come across the Tommy mobile flame-throwers based on their personnel-carrier, the Bren. I'm afraid a couple of my old comrades got rather burnt-up about them in '43 in Italy – please forgive the horrible pun.' He smiled winningly at the still-puzzled Wotan men. 'However, the trouble with such devices has always been the vulnerability of the operator. Mobile or not he has never been able to defend himself. But this Tommy secret weapon is different. It can fight back.' He reached up and slapped the tank's cannon with his cane.

'Do you mean to say that . . . that's a flame-thrower?' Schulze stuttered.

'Exactly, my big friend,' One-Flipper replied. 'This is the weapon with which we're going to make the breakthrough. Cinders, come on out of your hiding place and tell the gentlemen how our toy works . . .'

THREE

All the rest of that morning, Cinders, an ancient one-eyed corporal from a *Wehrmacht* tank unit, whose face was as black as his tanker's uniform, instructed them in the workings of the British secret weapon, in which One-Flipper Flosse seemed to set much store. He explained to them how the trailer contained some twelve hundred litres of a highly inflammable petrol mixture, which was pressured by cylinders of nitrogen gas also included in the trailer. This passed through the armoured pipe which linked the trailer with the tank, and ran to the ugly little firing nozzle where the co-driver's machine gun should have been. Here it was ignited – 'testing the spark', Cinders called it – and sent out a stream of flame some seventy-five metres long. 'Toast the eggs off'n elephant, that flame would,' he wheezed happily. 'But you've got to watch it. While you're flaming *them*, some nasty Ivan T-34 might just creep up and – ' he paused in his lecture and looked around at the circle of faces – 'give you a nasty surprise up the arse. And I'll tell yer this for free. When these Tommy Churchills are hit, three times outa five they go up in flames. Tommy cookers we used to call them in the old days. And then you've got exactly ten seconds to bale out before the flames come up from the engine compartment to the turret.'

'Happy old arsehole, ain't he?' Matz commented as the lecturer proceeded with the grim details of the terrible English secret weapon.

'Yeah,' Schulze agreed, 'a smile a second, that one.' He pulled out one of the foreign cigarettes and was about to light it, then he changed his mind hastily and stuck the unlit cigarette behind his right ear. 'What do you make of it then, Matzi?'

'Well, for one, we've put our dirty big dice-beakers in it.'

'Agreed,' Schulze said grimly, knowing that he had indeed volunteered what was left of Wotan for something very dangerous.

'Second, it's important.'

'Agreed again. Why else the Tommy toy?'

'Third, it's something to do with the Popovs. That Cinders up there just mentioned the T-34. So it stands to reason, we're going East once agen.'

'Yes, my little crippled genius, I agree with you once more. *And?*'

'Fourth, Schulzi, I think I'm going to make an immediate request for a transfer to the permanent staff here. I've got a peg-leg like the rest of 'em have. Why shouldn't I have it easy for once, eh?'

But that wasn't to be.

That same afternoon, One-Flipper Flosse led a little convoy of Wotan men out to one of Berlin's bomb-battered suburbs for a demonstration of the Crocodile's powers. Assembling the troopers on a small hill of brick rubble, which had once been the area's local savings bank, he announced: 'Gentlemen, now you'll see just what kind of weapon you will have at your disposal for the coming operation.' He nodded at Cinders who was to operate the flame-thrower while one of the Wotan men drove the Crocodile, 'All right, my black-faced friend – take her away!'

There was a little burst of flame like a match being struck, which they now knew meant that Cinders was testing the spark. Below him the driver let out the first of his many gears and the forty-tonner started to lumber forward, while the men on the heap of rubble watched intently.

'First target,' One-Flipper Flosse announced above the rattle tracks, 'that *Littfasssaule*[1] at ten o'clock. Imagine it's an enemy bunker.'

Abruptly there was a vicious hiss. A thick, burning yellow rod of flame spurted out from the ugly nozzle of the flame-thrower. Out and out, up and up it went, with a noise like someone wielding a thick leather strap. Suddenly the rod curved. Burning particles of oil splattered everywhere in ugly gobs. *Smack!* It hit the round concrete pillar with an ugly sound. A dozen yellow fingers leapt at the point of impact, probing wildly for cracks, holes, apertures into which they could insert themselves. In an instant the pillar was engulfed in a murderous roaring sea of flame, which fell away a moment later with an ugly belching sound to leave behind a cloud of strange-smelling, grey-black smoke.

'Bit high,' One-Flipper commented drily, while those of the Wotan who had never seen a flame-thrower in operation before stared at the blackened smoking concrete pillar with awed looks. 'Try for the slit at the top, Cinders.'

The grumpy veteran fired once more. Smacking, roaring, belching like some primeval dragon, the tongue of flame shot

[1] A round high concrete pillar used in big German cities for advertising posters.

out once again. Cinders hit the hole. The flame hissed through it, fanning out on the other side like some monstrous blow-torch, burning away the snow in its path and sending steam bursting up waist high.

'Holy strawsack!' Matz breathed. 'That would have given any poor shit in there a couple of hard-boiled eggs!'

'That it would,' One-Flipper agreed happily. 'But, my dear Corporal, you have seen nothing yet.'

As if in response to an unspoken signal, the driver started to move his vehicle forward once more, sending up little flurries of churned snow to his rear. It paused in front of what had once been a sewer, opened up by the RAF's bombs.

'A trench – an enemy trench!' One-Flipper yelled above the metallic racket.

Cinders fired. The flame shot the length of the sewer, bouncing from side to side along the shattered concrete pipe and then went bursting right round a bend in it. If it had been a real trench, anyone attempting to hide from that terrifying weapon would have had no chance whatsoever.

The Crocodile rattled on. It advanced on some ruined houses, their shattered windows and doors battened up with sheets of corrugated iron to keep out looters and children. It halted momentarily. Cinders fired. The flame poured out for ten seconds or more, drumming on the iron like thunder. They turned a dull purple and then a glowing crimson. The sheets visibly started to buckle. Next instant, the awed and frightened Wotan ducked as the sheets started to sail through the air above their heads.

One-Flipper showed his amusement. 'Rather fun, what?' he said, mimicking the affected tones of some Imperial Guards' lieutenant. Then his voice hardened again. 'Now old Cinders will show you his *pièce de résistance.* A very tough one, this one. A wet shot.'

The Crocodile moved on to another ruined brick house, probably some pre-war villa owned by some fat, prosperous middle-class businessman, now long abandoned. Again Cinders fired, but this time there was no yellow rod of flame. Instead, a stream of colourless liquid drenched the bottom storey of the ruin, running down the brickwork to form little stinking pools in the snow below, until the whole front of the villa was saturated. Finally Cinders flamed the structure.

The whole façade went up in one great cyclone of fiery-red flame, making the spectators leap back hurriedly as a wave of burning heat struck them. The pale winter sun was momentarily blacked out by the tremendous cloud of smoke and then, when it cleared, they could see that the whole front was a smoking, charred black and that everywhere the flame had touched there was a loathsome silvery film, like that left behind by some monstrous snail.

'Well, what do you think now, Sergeant-Major, eh?' One-Flipper Flosse asked as the Crocodile rattled off, leaving little flames flickering on the house-front. 'Not bad for a bunch of tin-cans? I think one could safely say that Battle-Group Flosse won't do too badly when the day comes, what?'

'And when will that day be, sir?' Schulze asked grimly, trying to shake off the little spot of burning liquid which clung to his right dice-beaker.

'War, as a veteran like yourself knows well enough, is composed of ten per cent action and ninety per cent inaction. We will wait until we receive our orders from that exalted person above.' One-Flipper Flosse pointed his malacca cane upwards at the hard, blue winter sky, as if he were indicating God himself. 'But somehow or other, my dear Sergeant-Major, I doubt we will be kept waiting very long.' And with that he was gone, limping quickly across the frozen snow, casting a dark dangerous shadow in front of him, leaving Schulze staring down at that little flame flickering still on his boot . . .

FOUR

The call to action came sooner than the men of Wotan expected. At midnight on their fourth day in the *Leibstandarte*'s former barracks, One-Flipper Flosse appeared personally in Schulze's room and, checking that the blackout was up, switched on the lights.

'Who the shitting hell – ' Schulze began, roused from a deep sleep, in which he was dreaming of a rather torrid incident with two whores and a midget of indeterminate sex which occurred recently on the *Reeperbahn*, before he realized that Flosse himself was standing there, dressed in full marching order, complete with pistol, machine pistol and pack. '*Sir?*'

'Out of that pit, Schulze,' One-Flipper commanded, the usual flippant tone gone from his voice. 'We've got our orders. We load our vehicles at the local goods station at exactly zero two hundred hours. The special is already there. Rouse the men. The base stallions have got the goulash cannon going. There'll be a hot meal and nigger sweat for them at zero one hundred. Motor march to commence at zero one-thirty precisely. Now hands off it, Schulze, and on with yer socks.' And with that he was gone.

The next hour passed in frenzied activity. Schulze roused the men and started them loading their gear and then, old soldier that he was, he hurried over to the wet canteen, smashed the lock with a quick burst of his Schmeisser – the noise was drowned by the roar of tank motors outside – and grabbed as many bottles of schnapps as he could lay his hands on, muttering to himself as he did so, 'Up the cups, it's gonna be a cold night.'

At one o'clock he supervised the kitchen bulls as they doled out the usual 'giddi-up' goulash, reputedly made of old nags, and the 'nigger sweat', an ersatz coffee produced from ground acorns, then partaking himself of a liquid breakfast, he reported to One-Flipper.

The officer was busily engaged poring over a map, but when Schulze entered he hastily folded it up, but not before Schulze's keen gaze had caught its title, '*General Staff Map – East Prussia*'. 'All ready to move off, sir,' he announced.

One-Flipper caught a whiff of his breath and said, 'Sergeant-Major, no naked flames within fifty metres of that flag you're flying at the moment or you'll go up like a light.' He grinned. 'Here,' he fumbled with that malacca cane of his and produced a small packet of sweets, 'cachous', he said. 'Better eat one of those. I don't want any outsider to think that Battle-Group Flosse goes off to war sauced-up.'

'And who might see us off at this godforsaken hour, sir?' Schulze grumbled, but he accepted the sweets all the same.

Thirty minutes later the blacked-out convoy, with the Crocodile in the lead, was rumbling through the deserted streets, shepherded by two fussy dispatch-riders, the only sign of their passing their dim-red convoy lights.

But if the streets were deserted, the station wasn't. At least a company of People's Guards was present, elderly but alert with their captured French rifles, sealing off the whole place, while inside the place itself the train of flat cars was already there with steam up, the flak crew at their posts on the quadruple flak cannon. Schulze looked at Matz significantly, but said nothing.

One-Flipper gave them no time to ponder the reason for the security measures, which seemed excessive for such a small unit. He was here, there and everywhere; limping hastily up and down the debris-littered platform; supervising the loading of the armoured vehicles; ensuring that the Wotan men who were to act as partisan lookouts at the end of each car had the extra thick winter gear and the normal leather face-masks; making sure that the MG 42 was set up on the flat car that would proceed the locomotive itself and promising the volunteers who would man it (for the flat car was there to ensure that if the track were mined, it would take the impact of the explosion and not the locomotive) an extra ration of hot coffee and schnapps every four hours. In spite of his normal languid, somewhat cynical manner, One-Flipper Flosse seemed to be a veritable dynamo of energy this morning, even Schulze had to admit that. Just before the train was about to leave, Schulze's attention was caught by the appearance of a small group of officers at the far end of the platform in the long grey coats of the General SS. As One-Flipper Flosse had predicted when he handed him the cachous, someone had come to see them off after all. But who?

Leaving Cinders to supervise the final chaining-down of his precious Crocodile in the last flat-car, Schulze nudged Matz, who was busy hiding their supply of schnapps in the little stinking *abort* at the end of their carriage. 'Come on, peg-leg,' he hissed. 'Let's go and have a look-see.'

'What's it to us?' Matz grumbled, fearing that during his absence some other cunning sauce-hound might get to the hidden drink.

'I like to know what we're getting into. I want to be prepared when the shit hits the fan,' Schulze said. 'Come on.'

Feigning preoccupied officiousness, the two NCOs strode down the length of the train, barking out orders, cursing slow soldiers and generally playing the role of a typical SS non-commissioned-officer, getting ever closer to the little group of officers, standing under the dim blue-light outside the Army Movements Office, with an attentive One-Flipper Flosse in their midst. Their voices were low and urgent, and Schulze, his back to them, could hear nothing of what they were saying because of the noise of the chains and the steam coming from the impatient locomotive. But at his side Matz, who had turned round in their direction, apparently to chivvy a slow trooper, did not need to hear a word; one glance at the skinny, bespectacled officer standing next to One-Flipper sufficed. He gasped audibly and tugged urgently at Schulze's sleeve. 'Turn round slow and gentle-like, Schulze,' he whispered. 'Cos they're looking this way.'

Schulze did as he was ordered. Then he too gasped when he saw that deathly pale face and those familiar pince-nez, which were blank in the light, looking as if there were no eyes in the sockets behind them. 'Great buckets of shit,' he gulped. '*Him!* What in three devils' name has Wotan got itself into now?'

'You can say that again, Schulze! What the hell have we gone and got ourselves into?'

The man standing under the blue light was none other than the most feared German in Europe: *Reichsführer der SS* Heinrich Himmler!

FIVE

As the slow, heavy train chugged at twenty kilometres an hour through the desolate snowbound winter countryside, those off-duty slept, save those like Schulze and Matz who had laid in a supply of schnapps. Now those few peered through the gaps in the boarded-up windows and periodically took sips at their bottles, trying to get warm in the freezingly cold wooden-seated compartments.

'As I see it, Matzi,' Schulze said, as he removed the dirt from behind his finger-nails with his bayonet, 'we're on a big one. Why else the flame-thrower, this special train, the gear we've got and now the big animal himself, Himmler, to speed us on our way?' He grunted and dug out what looked to Matz like a hundredweight of dirt from beneath his thumb-nail. 'We're pissing with the big dogs on this one, Matzi, mark my words.'

'You might be right, Schulzi,' Matz agreed gloomily, taking a gulp of his precious *Korn*.

'And when you piss with the big dogs, Matzi,' Schulze continued, 'it means only one thing.'

'Ascension Day commando?'

'Exactly, my tame little cripple. A one-way ticket skywards.'

'Well, you might be right that we're pissing with the big dogs on this one.' It was One-Flipper Flosse standing in the entrance to the compartment, his black cane carried across his shoulder like a rifle. He shook his head to indicate that they need not rise and stand to attention, knowing quite well that two old heads like Matz and Schulze wouldn't anyway. 'But you're wrong about the other part.' The amused smile vanished from the officer's face. 'This is 1945 and not 1940. There have been enough Ascension Day commandos – there'll be no more as far as Battle-Group Flosse is concerned. Now cover up those bottles and report to my compartment in ten minutes. I want to brief you on the mission.'

One-Flipper unscrewed the silver container at the head of his remarkable cane, deposited it on the wooden seat next to him, and contrived to pour a little stream of powder from the shaft on to the palm of his hand. 'Like a snort before we begin?' he enquired. 'Started it back in forty-four after the bone-merchants had worked me over. Got quite attached to the stuff.'

'What is it, sir?' Schulze enquired, puzzled.

'Coke – cocaine to you,' the officer replied.

Hastily Schulze shook his head and Matz shot him a quick glance. 'What kind of lulu is this?' it read, 'an officer on coke!'

One-Flipper Flosse shrugged easily and placing a small pinch of the drug in each nostril, snifted hard. He beamed at them. 'I'm not a real coke-head, you know. But alcohol does get boring after a while, doesn't it?' he drawled, as if it were the most natural thing in the world for an officer to be taking drugs. 'Now then to business. As my two senior NCOs, you obviously want to know where we're going. I'll tell you – '

'East Prussia,' Schulze beat him to it.

The officer laughed. 'You saw the map, didn't you, you big rogue?'

'Yes, sir.'

'Well, you saw right. East Prussia it is.'

THE EASTERN FRONT JANUARY 1945 (NORTHERN SECTOR)

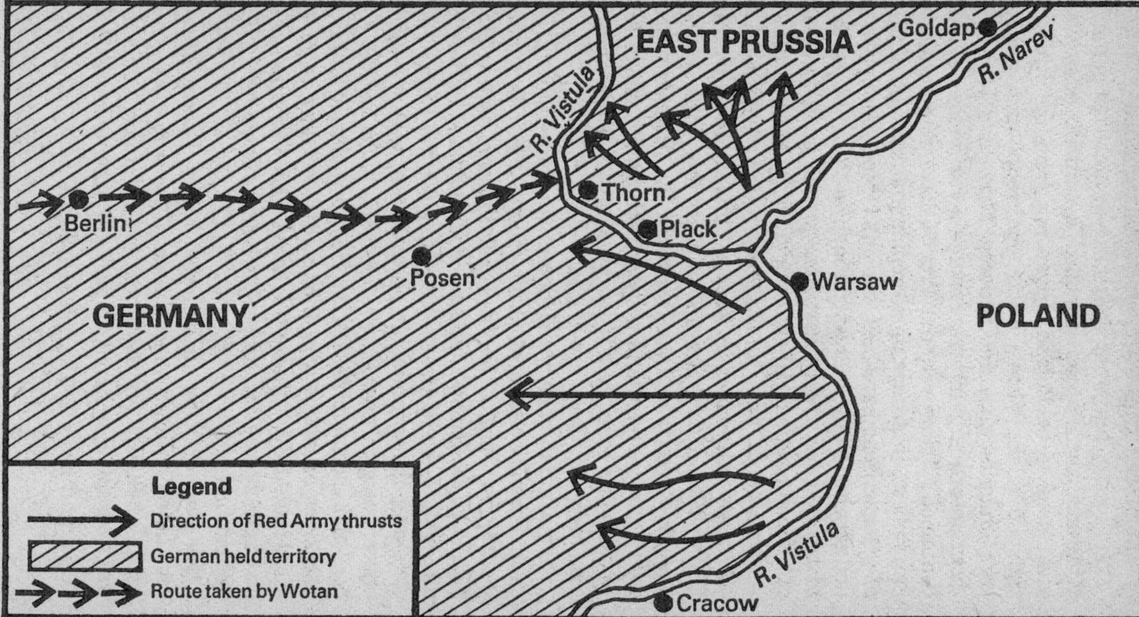

'It's all quiet up there, sir?' Matz queried.

'It is now, but while you chaps were having fun in the Ardennes, the Popovs launched a surprise offensive from what used to be Poland, advancing from the River Narev right up to the Vistula where our troops managed to hold them, roughly on a line between Thorn and Plack.' He let them absorb that information for a few moments and then continued: 'However, the Popovs have dug themselves in everywhere, in groups up to regimental strength, and scores of our garrisons have been cut off. Unfortunately we've just not got the troops to break through to them. Those old boys of the People's Guard battalions are no good for that kind of offensive action. All right for pissing against sentry boxes – that's about all.' He smiled at them winningly. 'Now you might ask yourselves what has this got to do with Battle-Group Flosse, eh?' Schulze said nothing. He could see the dope was already beginning to work. One-Flipper's eyes were starting to contract, and he kept rubbing the end of his nose with his one hand, as if it irritated him. 'I'll tell you. Spread that map out, Sergeant-Major.'

Schulze did as he was ordered, spreading out the map of East Prussia which he had caught the officer studying secretly in Berlin. Swiftly One-Flipper sketched in the details of the Russian advance out of Poland, indicating the direction of the main attack heading for the River Oder and once over that presumably on to Berlin, with the secondary attack going in through East Prussia, to its capital Königsberg and thence to the Baltic. He did it clearly and expertly like a senior officer who was used to briefing large groups of soldiers. Idly, Schulze wondered what One-Flipper's rank had been before the scandal, whatever it might have been, had occurred.

He paused. 'Now in this area below Thorn, just to the east of the Vistula, the Russians are apparently massing again, obviously for their next major attack. According to the spies of Foreign Armies East,[1] their Guard Army is

[1] German Military Intelligence in the East.

expected to attempt a crossing of the Vistula on thirtieth of January, exactly ten days from now.'

His face lit up as if at a joke. 'Now, of course, don't think that Battle-Group Flosse is expected to stop a Popov Guards Army. Oh no!'

The two NCOs said nothing; the thought hadn't even entered their heads, but obviously the officer, high now on drugs, was letting his mind run away with him, as was customary with addicts.

'We have a much more insignificant mission.' One-Flipper poked the map below Thorn with his cane. 'The little village of Neustedt – that's our objective. According to Intelligence, it is surrounded and cut off from the river by a battalion of Siberian riflemen. It will be our task to break through that ring and enter Neustedt.'

'And to what purpose, sir?' Schulze asked coldly, worried a little at the effect of the drug on the officer. What was he going to be like in action if he went in doped up like this?

'To what purpose?' One-Flipper Flosse echoed his question excitedly. 'I'll tell you. To bring out several cases of documents and books, plus half a dozen field-mattresses[1] who will be undoubtedly old, ugly and well-worn!' He laughed at his own humour.

Schulze and Matz stared at him incredulously. 'You mean, sir,' Matz stuttered, 'that we're expected to take on a whole battalion of slant-eyed Soviets in order to collect some books – and some field-grey horizontals?'

'I do indeed!'

'Well, I'll be sugared! They can't have all their cups in their cupboard in Berlin sending us off – '

With a raised cane, the officer stopped Matz's angry outburst. 'Ah, but my dear one-legged Corporal, although I indeed agree that they haven't got all their cups in the cupboard in Berlin, these are not just everyday books and papers.'

[1] Derogatory name given to female auxiliaries working with the German services.

'Well what are they then?' Schulze grumbled.

'The papers of Reich Marshal Hermann Goering!'

'Fat Hermann's?' Matz cried.

'Exactly. And do you know why they are important?' Both Schulze and Matz shook their heads in unison like stupid schoolchildren. 'Then I'll tell you. Because friend Fat Hermann has certain pretensions of glory, which do not fit in with the plans of *Reichsführer der SS* Himmler.'

'Don't understand,' Schulze snapped, getting irritated now by the drug-addict's manner. 'Don't understand at all.'

'Ours is not to reason why,' One-Flipper Flosse declaimed in English, 'ours is to do and die.'

'I don't shitting well speak Frog,' Schulze said. 'Let's have it in clear-text, Lieutenant. The lives of my boys are involved. I'm not gonna let them go hop for some sort of golden pheasant game.'

'How well you express yourself, Sergeant-Major,' One-Flipper said dreamily. 'There speaks the man of the people. What did Luther say: "Copy from the common man's mouth – "'

'Luther can go and snake himself,' Schulze interrupted crudely. 'Get on with it. The papers!'

'Oh yes, the celebrated papers.' One-Flipper's voice hardened and he seemed almost normal again. The Führer, as you perhaps know, had a bad shock last year – '

'You mean the attempt on his life?' Matz asked.

'Exactly. Well, his health is not of the best. Now there is the question of who will succeed him when the appropriate time comes.'

'Goering or Himmler?' Schulze said.

'*Klar.* So now the two of them are angling for position. Goering is his official successor, but he no longer has any muscle. Himmler, for his part, has the police apparatus and naturally the Armed SS at his command. But still Goering is the legal successor to the throne. Now our friend the Reichsheini[1] wants some dirt to throw at Fat Herman.'

[1] Slang name for Himmler.

'And those books, papers, etc., are to provide it,' Schulze said hastily.

'Yes. They are Fat Hermann's personal records, war diaries from the last three years. His staff of field-mattresses, guarded by a company of the Hermann Goering Division, were bringing them back to the *Karinhalle*[1] for safe-keeping when they got caught with their knickers down by the Popovs at Neustedt. Himmler thinks they'll provide him with the material he needs to blacken friend Hermann's image with the Greatest Captain of All Ages.' He said the words as if they were in capitals. 'It's our task to get them out – and the field-mattresses – before the new Popov offensive.'

Matz and Schulze looked at the officer aghast. 'Do you . . . you mean, that our lives are to be risked,' Schulze stuttered, his big face suddenly crimson with rage, 'so that four-eyed shit can get something on Fat Hermann – a kind of blackmail?'

One-Flipper Flosse nodded, the drug-induced animation beginning to leave his face now, being replaced by a look of depression, even despair.

'But it can't be true.' Schulze pulled himself together. After all the one-armed man facing him was an officer. 'Surely you as an officer could refuse that kind of mission, sir?' he said, his voice under control once more. 'It's not right to have good men sacrifice their lives for some kind of power struggle. Even Himmler hasn't got that kind of power . . .' His voice trailed away, as the new look in One-Flipper's eyes told him that the *Reichsführer der SS* had that kind of power.

'Himmler can do with us what he likes,' Flosse said softly, his voice without emotion. 'Perhaps you've been too long at the front, Schulze, to know what things are like at home. He can crush us underfoot – like ants. Once I thought you could refuse one of his orders, but I soon learnt that . . .'

It was at that moment that there was the crump of

[1] Goering's palace in Prussia, named after his first wife Karin.

explosive and the troop train was shuddering to a halt, with excited voices crying in alarm, '*Attack . . . attack . . . Partisan attack . . .*' The MG 42 on the front car started to hiss and in an instant all was excited confusion. *Wotan had run into trouble once more!*

SIX

'Fire!' One-Flipper Flosse yelled frantically, as followed by Schulze he clambered over the heaped coal of the tender and dropped into the cab, where the fireman lay in a groaning heap on the floor. 'Fire, you pack of stupid oafs! *FIRE!*'

On the coals, Schulze knelt and fired a quick burst at the white-clad figures appearing out of the fir woods on both sides of the stalled train. The gunners manning the MG 42 in front of the locomotive fed a new belt into their weapon and joined in. All along the line of carriages, the Wotan started tearing away the boards covering the windows and did the same.

Matz dropped next to Schulze. 'What gives?' he panted.

'Popov ski troopers,' Schulze answered and loosed off another wild burst at the men running clumsily across the snow towards them, firing as they came.

'Popovs – this far into Germany?'

'Well, they certainly ain't Father Christmas come to bring us a shitting present,' Schulze yelled above the chatter of the MG 42 and ducked as a burst of fire ran the length of the tender.

The Russians were only fifty metres away now. They were taking casualties, heavy casualties, the snowfield behind them was littered with white-clad dead and dying, but still they came on, stumbling and toppling as they were hit too, faces flung upwards in agony, frantic hands clawing the grey sky as if they were climbing a ladder. Schulze spotted two of them towing an old-fashioned Russian machine gun mounted on wheels. He knew the weapon. It was slow but effective and its gunners were protected by a metal shield. Once they got in position behind it, there would be trouble. He did not hesitate. Raising himself to his full height, ignoring the fire which was directed at him immediately, he tugged the stick grenade out of his boot. With a grunt he pulled the china cord and flung it. It sailed through the air and landed to their front. They were just a fraction too slow in throwing themselves to the snow. It exploded with an ugly thick crump and red flame spurted up. When it had cleared, both men lay dead near their buckled machine gun and one man's severed head was rolling back down the slope over which they had come.

The destruction of the machine gun seemed somehow to signal the end of the surprise attack. Sliding, running, screaming, jostling each other wildly to escape the murderous Wotan fire, the survivors streamed back to the cover of the woods. An instant later the firs had swallowed them up and their own fire was beginning to peter away.

One-Flipper didn't give the sweating Wotan men much time to compliment themselves on having beaten off the surprise ambush. Almost immediately, Schmeisser still smoking in his hand, he started to rap out orders. 'Matz, get rid of the stiff – ' he indicated the dead fireman – 'and see what you can do about him.' He pointed his Schmeisser at the elderly white-faced driver, who leant weakly against the cab where the first round of the Russian bazooka had struck it. 'Give him some of your firewater or something, but get him to pull himself together – quick . . . You, Schulze.'

'Sir!'

'With me. At the double.' He dropped awkwardly to the snow and, followed by Schulze, started to crunch across the field to where the first of the dead Russian ski-troopers lay, the smell of cordite hanging above them, sweet and sickly like that of a cheap woman's face powder.

With his foot he turned over the first man. He had been

hit in the stomach by a burst from the MG 42 and, as One-Flipper turned him over, his intestines slid slowly out of the dead man's ruined guts like some obscene, loathsome snake.

Schulze flinched, but One-Flipper didn't hesitate. Bending down, he fumbled with his one hand at the dead man's smock, opening it slightly to reveal the field-grey tunic beneath. 'Shit!' the officer cursed angrily. 'Now the clock really strikes thirteen!'

Schulze whistled softly through his front teeth. 'He's wearing German uniform, sir,' he said uncertainly.

One-Flipper straightened up. 'Of course he is,' he snapped. 'What did you expect him to be wearing? – black stockings and silk knickers! He's from the Seydlitz Army.' One-Flipper strode to the next man crumpled dramatically in the snow, machine pistol clutched tightly in his lifeless hands, and repeated the same check. Again a field-grey *Wehrmacht* uniform was revealed beneath the white ski-smock.

'But what is the Seydlitz Army, sir?' Schulze asked.

For a moment the officer did not reply. Instead he stared at the corpse-littered field towards the silent mysterious fir forest, as if he could see things there, known only to him. 'Patriots – or renegades,' he said finally in a low voice.

'German?'

'Oh yes, German all right,' One-Flipper said a little bitterly. 'In 1942, when Stalingrad surrendered to the Popovs, General von Seydlitz, a scion of an old Prussian military family, went into the bag with Paulus,[1] together with a dozen other senior generals. All of them were pretty unhappy about having been left out on a limb at Stalingrad, ordered by the Führer to fight to the last there and not make an attempt to fight their way back to our own lines. I should guess they thought they had been sacrificed. Perhaps they had. At all events, several of them were suborned to the Popov cause in forty-three and the so-called van Sedylitz Army formed.'

'Army?' Schulze queried, looking down at the dead men

[1] Commander of the encircled Army at Stalingrad.

and wondering what degree of hate would make German fight against German and die like this, as an enemy in one's own country.

'Well, at first the Seydlitz men engaged mainly in broadcasting propaganda messages to our own troops in the line. You know the sort of thing? Come over to Uncle Joe Stalin and there'll be steak for breakfast every morning and hot-assed Popov girls in every soldier's bunk. But seemingly Seydlitz is ambitious. Last year the first von Seydlitz combat units were formed and started to appear at the front. Mostly the Popovs have used them for ops behind our lines. They're ideally suited for the job. They're experienced soldiers, speak the lingo and know the country perfectly. What more could the Popovs want?'

Schulze nodded his understanding. Behind them the train was beginning to get up steam again and they could hear the rasp of a shovel digging out coal in the tender. Obviously Matz had found a substitute fireman. 'But how does this concern us, sir?' he asked.

One-Flipper hesitated momentarily. 'Well, if these Seydlitz people were here by chance, some twenty kilometres behind our front, all well and good. But twenty kilometres is a pretty deep long-range penetration mission, it seems to me. Could it be they knew we were coming? Could it be too that they know about the Goering papers and want their own people to lay their dirty paws upon them?'

'For what purpose?'

'The same as Himmler's – propaganda. Could it be possible that they are trying to hold us up so that their own Siberians at Neustedt can attack and capture the documents? Perhaps there is some dirt on Fat Hermann in them that they could use against the Reich.' He shrugged. 'These days everything is possible and most things probable.'

Schulze shrugged carelessly. 'So what, sir? Between us parson's daughters we can talk real German. Why should we risk our lives for the Reichsheini? Let the Popovs have the papers. Me, I could stand an extended stay in Berlin again, let's say for the next thousand years.'

'It's not quite as easy as that, Schulze, though I agree with you about the papers.'

'What do you mean, sir?'

One-Flipper Flosse looked at the big NCO thoughtfully and said, 'You're a Hamburger, you must have heard of Neuengamme?'

'Sure,' Schulze replied, puzzled by the question. 'It's up near the Elbe in the "Four Lands" area. I've not been up there since I was a kid. They used to grow a lot of fruit up there. We'd organize apples and pears from the trees when the shitty-booted farmers weren't looking.'

'That's the place,' One-Flipper said gloomily. 'Only these days they don't grow things there, *they kill them*!'

'What, sir? I don't understand.'

'Neuengamme now houses a camp for political prisoners.' The officer's voice grew harsh. 'In clear text – a concentration camp. And my wife's in it! That's why I've got to get my hands on those damned Goering documents.' Leaving Schulze no time to recover from his surprise, One-Flipper rapped out, 'Ten kilometres down the line, according to my map, there is a small country station. Now this is what we're going to do . . .'

Five minutes later the train of flat-cars was chugging on its way again, heading steadily eastwards trailing a black cloud of smoke behind it in the leaden sky, and deep in the forest, the patient observer started to spell out his message in broken Russian to the waiting operator, who would relay it to far-off Moscow . . .

SEVEN

The old man stuffed a cigarette in the bowl of his curved pipe, as was his wont, and lit the cigarette with a wrinkled hand, covered with brown liver spots. The man with the pince-nez waited, but he did not speak. With the old man one didn't speak until one was spoken to.

Outside in that monstrous square it was snowing. Great soft wet flakes falling on the skinny thickly-clad citizens, who trudged by without a glance upwards, their white-powdered shoulders bent, as if weighed down with the cares of centuries. The guards in their ankle-length greatcoats and fur coats, goose-stepping back and forth in front of the palace, seemed creatures from another and better world who would not deign to look at these miserable creatures who shared the square with them.

The old man breathed out a pleasurable cloud of blue smoke and pointed the meerschaum pipe at the nervous man with the pince-nez, whose bald pate gleamed a sickly yellow in the light of the great candelabra overhead, as if it were a weapon. 'Well, Lavrenti Pavlovich?' he demanded.

Beria, the Chief of the Secret Police, who ten years hence would be murdered in this very same room, pressed the pince-nez nervously to the bridge of his nose, unconsciously aping his greatest rival, Himmler. 'We think, comrade, that the papers will contain an account of his attempts to make a deal with the English,' he said.

'Through Dahlerus in 'thirty-nine?'

'No, comrade. *After* 'thirty-nine.'

The old man smiled. 'That would be interesting,' he said softly.

Encouraged by the old man's reaction, the Chief of Secret Police went on hurriedly. 'As you know, comrade, in 1939 Goering through the Swede Dahlerus tried to convince

Chamberlain not to declare war on the Fritzes.'

'And he failed, Lavrenti Pavlovich.'

'Exactly, comrade. In 1941 Hess tried the same thing –'

'And also failed,' the old man interrupted.

'Agreed, comrade. But this time it was different. The people that Hess went to see in England, he never saw. Churchill saw to that. He knew that any deal with the Fritzes on the part of those in England who wanted peace with them would mean he would have to go, perhaps even to that famous Tower of theirs in London. So Hess was snapped up, imprisoned and declared mad *before* he could meet those he had flown there to talk with.'

For the first time since Beria had made his appearance, the old man showed some interest. The Chief-of-Police was pleased with himself and continued hastily. 'But those people remained at large. Lords, fellow Conservative Party members, capitalists, people of that kind – they were too important for Churchill to have risked having them arrested for treason. It would have caused a scandal and might have prevented America from entering the war, something which Churchill needed desperately if England was going to survive. So this Hess group remained at large, and –'

'Goering took up the contact?'

'Just so, comrade.'

The old man sucked at his curved pipe, his leathery old face impassive, his dark oriental eyes revealing nothing. The Chief-of-Police waited patiently. The two of them had been associates ever since pre-revolutionary days, yet he still did not really know what went on in his boss's mind. All he knew was that he feared him in a way that he never feared any man in his whole life.

'When and where?' the old man asked at last.

'Stockholm in late 'forty-two and Ottawa the next year, probably in the spring. They used old friends of the fat one – Swedes – to do the job.'

'Do you think Churchill knew, Lavrenti Pavlovich?'

Beria shook his head. 'No, I don't think so. By 1943 the

war had turned and I think Churchill is too wise a bird to involve himself in such a business when he knew that Germany was beginning to be beaten.'

The old man nodded. 'Are we all to be betrayed by those who serve us?'

Beria did not know whether the question was rhetorical or not. In the end he decided it was not and said, 'You, dear comrade, will never be betrayed by those who serve you.'

'As long as they fear me enough, Lavrenti Pavlovich,' the old man chuckled, though there was no warmth in the laugh. 'So?'

'So, comrade, it is our thinking that if we can procure those papers and they contain what we suspect, they will bring about Churchill's downfall. Who will ever believe that he knew nothing of the dealings of his former colleagues and important Conservative Party members with the Fritzes, going back to the days of Hess in 'forty-one? It will mean a break with Roosevelt, who invariably suspects Churchill, and with your great ability, comrade, you will undoubtedly be able to deal with Roosevelt as you wish, once Churchill is out of the way.'

The old man nodded. 'Yes, Roosevelt is a fool, a provincial fool. He is more concerned with the results of some insignificant election in one of his states than the fate of the world. Churchill is different. He is a bold rogue, that one. He would have made an excellent member of the Central Committee.' For a moment or two the old man mused on that startling thought, then he asked: 'And what is being done to obtain these precious papers?'

'There is no escape from the place in which they are to be found. The Fritzes are surrounded there.'

'And why haven't they been captured already?'

'The defences have proved too difficult for our infantry. They have no heavy weapons to storm the place. They need tanks.'

The old man frowned, his eyes almost disappearing in a sea of wrinkles in that seamed leathery face of his. 'Then send tanks, a whole division of them if necessary.'

'The Stavka[1] has ordered them to move forward to the place.'

'It should have been done earlier. Time is of the essence, comrade.'

Beria blanched and felt the sweat break out unpleasantly all over his body. He knew what that change to 'comrade' meant; the old man was displeased. At any moment heads could begin to roll.

'We are confident, comrade,' he said hastily, 'that our tame Fritzes will hold them up.'

'Tame Fritzes?'

'The Seydlitz Army.'

'Ah, *those* Fritzes,' the old man said and puffed at his pipe, wreathing his face momentarily in a cloud of thick blue smoke. 'Are they to be trusted?'

'Yes, comrade, to the death,' Beria replied. 'There is nothing like a converted Fritz. I swear they are more loyal to the Party than – ' he caught himself in time. He had been about to say 'you', but that might have been dangerous – 'than I am. And as you know I have served the Party these thirty years or more.'

'Oh yes, we all know just how loyally you have served the Party,' the old man said.

Again Beria froze. With the old man one had always to be on the alert for the slightest change in his voice, the merest nuance, the faintest inflexion. What had it meant? Did he doubt his, Beria's, loyalty? Or was he confirming it?

'What is the plan for the Fritzes?' the old man continued, seemingly not noticing the fact that Beria's face was now streaming with sweat, although the big room was not overly heated.

'They are to destroy – or at least delay – the force which is attempting to relieve the place where the Goering papers are.'

'And if they don't?'

'They answer for it with their heads.'

'Good.' The old man took a deep draw at his pipe. 'Just

1 Soviet High Command.

one more thing, just to make certain. Let this General von Seydlitz lead in the tanks which will attack the place. It pleases me to think that Fritz will fight Fritz.'

'It will be done immediately, comrade.'

'And one other thing, Lavrenti Pavlovich.'

'Comrade.'

'Make him aware that *his* head also hangs in the balance if he fails.' He beamed at Beria. 'Now you may go.'

Hurriedly Beria left his presence, leaving him sitting there alone on his throne-like chair, puffing at his curved pipe, his brain racing, but his dark eyes and impassive wrinkled face revealing nothing.

Joseph Stalin was planning the fate of the world.

Two
Crocodile

ONE

'Here she comes, sir!' Schulze whispered urgently. One-Flipper raised his head slightly from beneath their cover under the snow-heavy pines overlooking the bridge which crossed the chasm below.

The train, which they had abandoned two hours earlier, just before dawn, was steaming bravely towards the bridge, trailing a bold flag of white smoke behind it.

'What do you think, Schulze?' One-Flipper asked urgently. 'Does it look all right to you?'

Schulze peered at the lumps covered by tarpaulins on the flat cars for a moment and then said, 'To my glassy orbs, they look real. I only hope that driver has done a bunk already. Because if he hasn't and you're right, sir, he's gonna get a nasty kick up the arse in a minute.'

One-Flipper squinted his eyes, searching the cab for any sign of the elderly driver. 'Visibility's clear enough, Schulze, but I can't make it out. Let's hope for the best.'

He fell silent and the two observers watched the long train chug ever closer to the trestle bridge in a tense silence. Now the only sound was the clatter of its wheels on the metal track and the hiss of escaping steam. Hastily Schulze ran his gaze around the surrounding area, but there was nothing but gleaming, still fields of snow, sparkling in the harsh winter sun. It looked as if they were alone in the world, apart from the train far below.

The flat car in front of the locomotive had begun to clatter on to the bridge, the wooden sleepers making a 'chunk-chunk' sound under its weight. Still nothing happened. Next to Schulze, One-Flipper bit his bottom lip in anger and frustration. Perhaps he had been too damn smart for his britches after all and this wasn't the spot!

The locomotive rattled on to the bridge. It was now or

never. One-Flipper felt his good hand clench into a nervous wet fist. *'Come on, you bastards!'* a little voice inside him screamed. *'Come on, do it now! NOW!'*

The locomotive was halfway across now, in a few moments the flat car would have reached the other side. Still nothing had happened. Next to the officer, Schulze wiped a big dirty paw across his suddenly parched lips. It was not going to happen as the officer had so confidently predicted.

Suddenly there was a faint rumble, which grew louder and louder by the instant. Puffs of smoke started to shoot from the trestles supporting the bridge. They began to shake like live things. Small, blue flames started running the length of the bridge and the centre began to bend. Abruptly the locomotive was attempting to run uphill and failing. There came a great metallic groaning sound from the central span.

One-Flipper punched Schulze excitedly on the arm. 'It's working!' he cried. 'It's working . . . I was right after all! Schulze – ' the rest of his words were drowned by a gross, obscene belch, as the main charge exploded. In an instant, the centre of the bridge was obscured by a great scarlet flame, through which the locomotive, its pistons clanging back and forth, rose high in the air, before turning a slow cartwheel and falling to the bottom of the chasm with a hellish rending crash. One by one, the coaches and flat cars behind it teetered at the edge of the gap torn in the centre of the bridge, before each one fall after the locomotive, like toys upset by some wanton child.

Schulze stared open-mouthed, as the sounds of that great crash echoed and re-echoed through the valley. Then the white-clad figures started to emerge from the surrounding trees to stare in silence at the jumbled metallic chaos below and he pulled himself together. Next to him a triumphant One-Flipper whispered, 'All right, Schulze, let's get out of here while the going's good.'

'Do you think those treacherous shits'll go down there to investigate?' Schulze asked, as they crawled backwards out of their cover.

'Doubt it. They've seen what they wanted to see – the train they attacked the other day well and truly derailed. Why should they examine the wreckage? After all we're still ten kilometres behind German lines and they can expect some sort of party to come up here soon and check it out. No, Schulze, their motto is probably, hit hard, hit fast, and then powder.' He straightened up, obviously highly pleased with himself. His plan to throw the traitors off their track had worked. Beneath those tarpaulins there was nothing except a heap of old packing cases and rusting boogies that they had assembled hastily during the night at the little wayside station where they had unloaded their armour at record speed. 'Now, you big rogue,' One-Flipper concluded, 'I think we'll make dust in very much the same way. Come on, let's go. It's a long way to Neustedt yet . . .'

They crawled along most of that long icy day. The leading Crocodile, driven now by Cinders, who protested that he was a gunner not a driver, could only make twenty kilometres an hour, even when the road was not uphill, and the rest of the long convoy of vehicles had to reduce their speed accordingly. Time and time again, an anxious One-Flipper standing in the freezing turret, face muffled in a leather mask, cast glances at the hard blue sky. But it was empty of enemy aircraft, although the Popovs had complete air superiority.

Twice they passed through the typical villages of the area, a collection of low thatched-roofed, brick-and-wattle structures, grouped around a small grey church. But in both cases they were empty, barn doors open, lean dogs picking around the farmyards trying to find something to eat, clear evidence that they had been evacuated hurriedly.

Schulze rubbed the end of his frostbitten nose grimly and remarked, 'Who would have thought it would have come to this, sir? The Popovs on German soil and our own stubble-hoppers fighting against us. What did we do wrong?'

One-Flipper looked down at a rag-doll, abandoned by

some panic-stricken girl, as the Crocodile's tracks crunched over it and pulped it to nothing. 'We did a lot wrong, Schulze – a hell of a lot! What do the peasants say? He who eats with the devil needs a long spoon. Ours was obviously not long enough.'

Schulze did not quite understand the meaning of the officer's statement, but he guessed that One-Flipper was no friend of the National Socialist creed. The man had been hurt and hurt bad, but how he did not know. He relapsed into silence and watched as the greedy black crows soared easily in the hard blue sky, circling the lean, skinny-ribbed dog in the snow below. Once it finally fell, they'd go for its eyes. Involuntarily he shuddered.

Time passed in leaden, freezing slowness. The whole countryside seemed abandoned, almost as if it had never been lived in. There was a brooding, frightening emptiness to it all, with nothing to be seen as far as the eye could see. Schulze, not normally a sensitive man, could sense that most of the Wotan men were similarly affected by that desolate winter landscape and he caught himself more than once doing exactly the same as they were doing: turning at regular intervals and looking backwards, as if they half-expected to see someone following them. 'Heaven, arse, and twine!' he cursed *sotto voce* to a frozen Matz. 'This place puts years on me. Let's hope we get to shitting civilization soon!'

Civilization came towards evening. The Crocodile was cautiously approaching a dark cluster of low houses which formed a village not marked on One-Flipper's map, when a tall figure startled them by appearing out of the evening gloom. At first they thought it was a woman, for the figure appeared to be in a long skirt of the kind worn by the peasants. Then they caught a glimpse of the white trimmings of the collar and Matz shouted, 'It's a sky pilot!'

'A what?' One-Flipper queried, bringing up his machine pistol carefully.

'A priest, sir. A Roman-candle sky pilot!'

The Crocodile slowly rattled to a stop in front of the strange figure. Behind them the rest of the vehicles did the same. The man in the cassock seemed in no way perturbed to see the column, which had appeared so suddenly out of nowhere. His hands thrust in the wide sleeves, so that he looked like a Chinese mandarin, he advanced towards the first tank, smiling broadly. 'Greet God, my sons!' he said, using the traditional greeting.

'When you see Him,' One-Flipper answered, using the equally traditional, if somewhat cynical, soldier's answer. 'Where have you suddenly popped up from, Father?'

The middle-aged priest beamed up at the officer. 'Why, from my village of course.' He indicated the huddle of little houses behind him. 'Where else?'

'I see. And is your village inhabited? Can we get something hot there?'

'No, I'm afraid not, my son,' the priest replied, beaming all the time, as if it gave him great pleasure to be standing out here in the middle of this snowbound nowhere with the freezing wind coming straight in from Siberia. 'They have all gone, my flock. They joined a trek a week ago, with all their seven things. Every man, woman and child.'

'And you? Why did you stay?'

The priest shrugged easily. 'Where should I go? There is death there,' he pointed to the west. 'There is death here. I stay with my church.'

One-Flipper absorbed the information. 'And German troops? Do you know where the nearest German troops are?'

'Not exactly, my son, but . . .' The priest went on to describe the local area, while Schulze studied him from the side. There was something odd about the priest, but he didn't put his finger on it till much later, and by then it was too late. 'So you see, Lieutenant,' the priest concluded his explanation, 'my guess is that the German – I mean, our front-line – is somewhere over there to the north-east, roughly in the area of Gross-Luetow.'

'Thank you.' One-Flipper pressed the throat-mike and growled, 'All right, Cinders, pull your digit out of that nasty orifice of yours. *Carbide!*'

Cinders understood the old SS expression for 'start-up'. Grumbling over the intercom, he engaged the Crocodile's first gear and the tank started to pull away. Hastily the priest sprang to one side and made the sign of the cross, crying above the clatter of the tracks, 'And God be with you, my sons!'

Thus he remained standing in the snowy ditch, making the sign of the cross over each vehicle as it roared past, ignoring the rude signs the battle-hardened vets of Wotan made to him, until he vanished in the growing dusk.

It was only when they had begun to crawl through the cobbled village square, its hard-packed snow-covering stained yellow with the urine of animals, past the little church with its large sign '*Evangelical-Lutheran Church*' that Schulze finally realized what was wrong. 'Shit on shingle, sir!' he bellowed, grabbing hold of One-Flipper's arm, 'that priest – he's really took us on the arm!'

'What do you mean – took us on the arm?' One-Flipper demanded, spinning round to face a confused, angry Schulze.

The big NCO could hardly get the words out, he was so enraged. 'That pious fart said . . . he was a Catholic priest, didn't he?'

'Yes, well?'

'And he said that that was . . . his church?'

'Yes, so?'

'Well, don't you see, sir?' Schulze exploded finally. 'That church is *Protestant*!'

One-Flipper Flosse hit his forehead with his one hand. 'Of course, Schulze . . . of course! Great balls of flying shit, we've been spotted again . . .'

TWO

'*The front!*' Schulze exclaimed, as the Crocodile rattled to a stop.

'The front indeed,' One-Flipper echoed. 'I know it well.' He stared up the cobbled snow-covered road, littered with battle-debris and on both sides dead cows, hugely inflated and giving off a nauseous stench.

Matz took his eyes off a skinny pig prodding its dead mate with its snout, and said: 'It's something I, for one, can do without. But where's the defence?'

'*Here!*'

All three standing in the turret swung round surprised, as the sudden voice continued with: 'One more minute and you'd have had a *panzerfaust*[1] up your arse – right quick!' An army lieutenant was crouched in the ditch behind them, a dwarf of a man, glaring at them through thick-lensed issue glasses in myopic rage, a *panzerfaust* held in delicate, if dirty hands.

Schulze smiled. In the heroic posters back home, the front-swine depicted never looked like that. There they were always gigantic heavy-muscled blond heroes. But this was the real thing – a dirty dwarf who looked like a solicitor's clerk suffering from piles and dandruff. 'Hold yer water, Lieutenant,' he said, 'we're friends.'

The lieutenant got slowly out of his ditch. 'Friends,' he growled. 'Never had a friend in my whole life. Why do you think I'm in this shit now, eh?' He advanced towards them and saw the fading SS runes on their collars. 'SS, eh. What kind of trouble are you pigs bringing me?'

'Not much, friend,' One-Flipper answered, dropping from

[1] Bazooka.

the turret. Swiftly he unscrewed the silver top of his cane and said, 'Have a snort.'

The bespectacled lieutenant accepted the drink without surprise; he looked like a man who could be surprised by nothing any more. 'Good stuff, that,' he gasped. 'Really zaps the tonsils. All right, what do you want?'

'Warmth, a place to sleep for the night – and information,' One-Flipper answered.

'I can give you number two. One doesn't exist any more. This is the shitting North Pole, you know. As for information, I can tell you, we're here and the Popovs are out there somewhere.' He pointed at the grey horizon. 'Where exactly, I'm not about to find out.'

One-Flipper absorbed the information and said, 'All right, where's our kip for the night?'

'Barn two o'clock,' the sour little officer replied. 'Approach it from the back. Five-minute intervals between vehicles. I don't want any Popovs spotting you and bringing down the artillery. No smoke after four o'clock and no noise after dark, and *please*, no usual SS heroics. Mrs Schmidt's ugly son – ' he pointed a mittened finger at his skinny weak chest – 'wants to live out the rest of the month of January. All right, I'll see you in ten minutes.'

One-Flipper grinned and clambered back on to the turret. A few seconds later they were rolling through the German lines – old men armed with French rifles, or skinny, pimply youths, shivering in foxholes on both sides of the little village road. 'Christ,' Matz exclaimed as he saw them, 'one good wet fart and the whole lot'd fall over!'

'That you can say again,' Schulze agreed. 'If this is all the Army's got left, Mother sell the pig and buy me out!'

Ten minutes later Battle-Group Flosse was safely accommodated in the animals' half of the big barn-cum-farmhouse, while the Wotan troopers busied themselves stripping wood from the ceiling and floor in order to make fires to cook their evening soup.

The little lieutenant watched them for a few moments

with professional interest, remarking several times, 'Remember, no smoke after four o'clock.' before turning to One-Flipper and saying, 'Another snort of that sauce of yours and I'll tell you what bit I know.'

One-Flipper obliged him with another drink and the lieutenant commenced his briefing. 'The front is everywhere and nowhere,' he said.

'What exactly do you mean?' One-Flipper asked.

'I mean there is no stable front. Sure the Ivans are out there, but exactly where I wouldn't know.'

'You mean you haven't run any patrols to find out?' One-Flipper asked incredulously.

The lieutenant looked at the SS officer, and slowly pulled down the corner of his right eyelid. 'Can you see any green there, friend? Patrols with the cannon-fodder I've got masquerading as infantry! You've got to be tired of life to pull one like that. All I know is that if you go up that road leading out of the village with those sardine cans of yours, sooner or later the Ivans are gonna to give it to you – and how!'

Borrowing One-Flipper's remarkable cane, the lieutenant sketched in two lines in the frozen dust at their feet. 'Here we are. This is the direct route to Neustedt, some ten kilometres from here. But you won't take that one, will you?'

One-Flipper shook his head. 'No, it would be too obvious and the Popovs would be expecting us.'

'Exactly.'

'So what do you suggest? Out there in the fields, the depth of the snow would slow my tanks down too much.'

The bespectacled lieutenant drew another line in the dust leading away from the other two lines. 'There's a kind of logging trail running from the village here. It runs up into the woods, and my guess is that it could well take you nearly all the way to Neustedt before the wood ends. The going's steep, but the trees should cover you and I should imagine that there'll be no Ivans in the woods themselves. Why should there be?'

One-Flipper looked interested. 'That might be it. Even

if the snow's deep up there and we're slowed down, we'll be protected from air attack by the cover of the trees.'

'Yes, that's my thinking. But there is one catch, comrade.'

'There always is,' One-Flipper replied, with that old cynical grin of his spreading across his face. 'It's been the story of my life.'

'Mine, too. That's why I'm freezing my arse off in this God-forsaken hole and not toasting my toes in some warm adjutant's office, back in the Reich. Now the catch.' He marked an 'X' near the line representing the logging trail. 'Just where the wood commences, there is a large house. Probably belonged to the local forester or something. It looks empty, but it isn't. The day before yesterday at dusk, I was watching it for any sign of life when I heard a sound I couldn't quite identify at first. Then I made it out. Somebody had sneaked out to piss in the snow – and the only people pissing out in the snow over there are Ivans. So it's occupied, though I still have to catch my first glimpse of one of the bastards.'

'Always have been cunning shits like that,' Schulze grunted. 'Ten times better than us at camouflage.'

The two officers nodded their agreement.

'So – ' One-Flipper began.

But the little lieutenant beat him to it. 'So, if any one of the Russkis holding that house manages to get away or contacts any other of their units, you're gonna to be caught up in those woods with your skivvies well and truly around your ankles, comrade.'

'We'll flame them, every single one of them,' One-Flipper said, no emotion in his voice at the mention of the terrible death he had planned for the unknown Russians.

'And how do you think you're going to get those tin cans of yours close to the house without the noise alerting the Ivans to what's coming their way, comrade?' the little lieutenant enquired. 'By the time you're in position to fire they'll have already been screaming down the field-phone for help for five minutes.'

One-Flipper looked grim. 'Dammit, but of course you're

right. Even if we croak them, the others will know we're heading for the forest.'

Schulze looked at Matz. 'Well?' he demanded.

Reluctantly his running-mate nodded.

'Sir,' Schulze said hesitantly.

'Yes,' One-Flipper said.

'Corporal Matz and I want to volunteer.'

One-Flipper looked at the big NCO sharply. 'Volunteer?'

'Volunteer?' the little lieutenant echoed. 'Am I hearing correctly? Did I hear someone say "*volunteer*"?' He grinned. 'I thought this was 1945, not 1940. Sergeant-Major, they ought to put up a statue to you in Berlin, with the words engraved beneath it, "Here stands a volunteer from the Greater German Army!"'

'Yes,' Matz said sourly, 'they probably will when we're looking at the potatoes from beneath after they've planted us.'

'Sir,' Schulze's voice rose, 'if we sneak out tonight, we could cut all their communication wires. The Popovs never do have much in the way of radio equipment anyway. Cut their telephone cables and then you can come in with that monster, making as much noise as you want.'

One-Flipper beamed at Schulze. 'There could be a bit of tin in this for you, Sergeant-Major.'

'I've got the set, sir,' Schulze sniffed. 'When do you want us to go?'

'Tomorrow morning. You can do your act as soon as Cinders has built up the pressure in the bottles and the Crocodile's ready for action. Now then –' he flicked a catch in the cane – 'what about a cigar?'

Next to Schulze, Matz said in a dying voice, 'Yeah, and I know the hole that cigar's going into – and it ain't the one I put my cake into . . .'

THREE

The sky was an inky black. Even the snow gave little light to the two men who crept cautiously out of the silent village and, with their sock-covered boots making hardly a sound on the frozen surface of the snow, began to make their way up the track towards the one-time forester's house.

Neither of them spoke. They were veterans and they'd done this kind of thing often enough before; all the same both of them had nerves which tingled with an almost unbearable excitement.

Matz took the lead, with Schulze coming up at the rear, machine pistol slung over his enormous back now, but with his 'Hamburger equalizer', a pair of brass knuckles, decorating his big right hand. If Matz ran into trouble, it would be his job to look after the little man and sort it out without alerting the rest of the enemy by using his machine pistol.

Now the squat shape of the forester's house, a harder black against the lighter one of the sky, started to loom up closer. Matz crossed the road to the line of trees which bordered it there. Careful not to disturb the snow which lay thick on their branches, he felt from tree to tree. Schulze waited in the shadows. He knew what the little corporal was looking for. Radio cable. The Ivans, cunning as they were, never strung it from tree to tree openly, as did German signallers. They always camouflaged it among the branches. Matz found nothing. He crossed to the other side of the road, Schulze watching not only him but the surrounding area – just in case, and continued his search there. Suddenly Schulze heard him grunt. He had found the cable. There was a tight soft snap as wire parted. Matz had begun cutting the multi-coloured cables.

Schulze licked parched lips, telling himself he was so dry because of the snow, but knowing, in truth, his thirst came from tension and not a little fear. If the two of them were caught out here in the open, they'd be for the chop. These days the Ivans did not take prisoners. He flashed a look at the house. It was silent. To any casual observer it appeared deserted, abandoned like so many houses in the area where the owners had fled before the advancing Russians. But he knew that was not the case, for he could now smell that typical Ivan stink: a mixture of manure, unwashed bodies and the coarse black tobacco the Russians smoked.

The seconds seemed to pass with leaden feet. Twice Schulze was tempted to tell Matz to hurry up, but he knew the little man was working as quickly as he could, taking care that he did not miss a wire: all their lives depended upon no message reaching the outside.

Finally Matz was finished. Breathing hard, he crossed to where Schulze was standing guard. 'Great balls of fire, Matzi,' Schulze growled under his breath, 'what the hell were you doing so long over there – having a bit of five against one?'

'Five against one, my arse, I – '

Matz never finished his angry reply, for in that moment a harsh guttural voice cried, '*Stoi!*' Next instant a thin beam of bright white light stabbed the darkness and blinded them.

Schulze reacted instinctively. His right foot lashed out. Matz yelped with pain as Schulze's big dice-beaker caught him on the shinbone of his good leg and he tumbled to the ground at the same moment that Schulze dived to the right. The burst of machine-pistol fire cut the air where they had just been standing and Schulze could feel the heat as the tracer hissed over his back. Matz rolled over, pulled the stick grenade from his belt and hurled it the best he could from the reclining position. It exploded at once in a scarlet blast of flame. Someone screamed and someone else shouted angrily in Russian.

The explosion gave Schulze the respite he needed. Ripping the machine pistol from his back, he fired a wild burst from left to right, still blinded by the sudden light and hoping that he was going to strike lucky.

He did. Alerted by the firing, but not knowing whether or not the cables had already been cut, One-Flipper, waiting in the turret of the Crocodile, yelled, 'All right, driver – *carbide!*'

The British tank lurched as the driver let out the clutch hurriedly. One-Flipper flung a hasty glance around the turret. The red light glowed on the firing circuit of the 75mm cannon. The shells in the racks had their clips off and were ready for firing. Down below in the green-glowing gloom, Cinders was in position at the flame gun. Everything seemed all right, though he knew they were taking a chance, operating the tank in darkness without infantry protection. Any sly Popov armed with a bazooka or a sticky mine could soon put an end to their little adventure if he could get close enough under the cover of darkness. But it was a risk they had to take.

Now they were approaching ever closer to the red zip of tracer, which indicated that Matz and Schulze were in trouble. Obviously they had heard the racket in the forester's house, but it remained as silent and dark as ever. One-Flipper had a sudden feeling of nakedness. Then it happened. Abruptly the front of the house crackled with flame. Slugs howled off the turret. Something slammed into the snow in front of the Crocodile. It reared up on its back bogies, shaking all over.

'The bastards have an anti-tank gun in there!' Cinders cried over the intercom.

'Yes – ' One-Flipper's reply was drowned by the impact of a shell striking the turret and skimming away with a frightening metallic howl. For a moment the inside wall glowed a dull red. One-Flipper gulped and pressed his throat-mike. 'Prepare to flame, Cinders!' he ordered.

Now they had passed the snap-and-crackle of the small-arms fight. The house was perhaps some three hundred metres away. One-Flipper knew that it was an extreme range for the flame gun, but he couldn't chance that anti-tank gun knocking them out. Another solid armour-piercing shell came rushing at them, a white blur in the darkness. He ducked instinctively as it slammed into the ground only metres away. 'Flame gun – *fire!*' he yelled.

Cinders needed no urging. He knew the danger they were in. The yellow rod of flame leapt out from the Crocodile. It rushed forward, roaring and rolling across the snow, making it hiss, turning night into day, and came to a stop just short of the house.

'Up ten metres, Cinders,' he roared over the intercom, as the anti-tank gun cracked again. 'In three devils' name – UP!'

The Crocodile smashed through a picket fence. Clods of mud and snow were flying up on both sides in a confused wake. Down below the Wotan driver kept wrenching the steer bar back and forth, trying to throw the Russian anti-tank gunners off their aim. One-Flipper was thrown back and forth, anxiously listening for that clatter from the bogies which would indicate they had thrown a track.

Cinders fired again. The flame swept forward, embraced the house in its deadly red grip and swept right up to the roof. In an instant the whole structure was burning, and hysterical human torches were tumbling out of doors and windows, fleeing across the fields, dragging flames behind them or writhing back and forth in the snow in their extreme agony, trying in vain to put out the flames. Down below the second gunner opened up with the co-axial machine gun. The fleeing men didn't get far. The burst at such close range blasted them off their feet and they went down in a wild twitching convulsive heap.

'Flame her again, sir?' Cinders' voice crackled across the intercom.

One-Flipper flung a quick glance at the fiercely burning forester's house and said in a suddenly hushed voice, as if he had realized for the first time just what a terrible fate he had condemned its inhabitants to, 'No, Cinders, I think that's enough . . .'

FOUR

Schulze, still bleeding on his left cheek where a Russian slug had nicked him, wandered through the smoking ruins. There were Russian dead everywhere, horribly charred and mutilated by that terrible weapon. The bodies seemed to have been blown back by the force of Crocodile's flame and lay in naked, blackened heaps. Some lay in fantastically contorted poses, as if the flame had frozen them thus, and all were minus everything save their helmets and boots, which gave them a ghastly, ridiculous appearance.

Matz took his eyes off what looked like a charred, shrivelled root of a tree, but which was in fact an arm, and said: 'Well, that shitting Tommy tank did for this lot all right, didn't it, Schulze?'

Schulze wanted to be sick, but instead he took a deep breath and growled, 'You can say that again, Matzi.' He looked down at a dead Russian, who stared up at him with black eyeballs, naked, charred and obscene. 'Poor shits. They never knew what hit them – '

'Well, what do you think?' One-Flipper's voice cut into his words. 'Do you think you found all the cables before the Popovs spotted you?'

'I think so, sir.'

'And there's no sign of a short-wave radio in this mess, sir,' Matz added. 'We've searched it pretty thoroughly.'

One-Flipper nodded his thanks and turned to see Cinders and the rest of Crocodile's crew pouring in the last of their fuel: sixteen hundred litres of a white treacly-looking liquid. 'The things man does to man,' he said softly, as if speaking to himself. Then he pulled himself together. 'All right, Sergeant-Major Schulze, you take one of the Skodas and get under way. We'll stay approximately one kilometre behind you. We'll keep in radio contact, channel open all the time, but no unnecessary talk, just in case the Popovs are monitoring our radio traffic in this area. We don't want to alert them to our presence in the woods. Clear?'

'Clear, sir.'

'Stop once you are about to clear the woods. I want to have a look-see at the Russian positions outside Neustedt personally. All right, don't take any unnecessary risks, keep your eyes skinned and your nose clean. Good luck.'

'Thank you, sir.' Both of them saluted, turned and crunched over the crisp hard snow to the first of the waiting Skoda self-propelled guns.

'All right, you bunch of wet-tails,' Schulze bellowed at the Wotan men staring down at him from the deck, 'you're being granted a very special honour today. Sergeant-Major Schulze is going to be conveyed in your vehicle. So get the lead out of yer arses and get this Czech clockwork toy of yours wound up and started.'

'Schulze on board,' someone out of sight below groaned. 'Now we're really in trouble!'

Hurriedly the crew scuttled to their tasks, while Schulze checked out the radio himself before letting the operator set the net. Then he unhooked one of the leather face-masks from the wall of the big open turret and slung it at Matz. 'We'll do ten-minute spells each, Matzi. You first and then me. And try to keep your glassy orbits open.' He stared ahead at the rigid ranks of snow-laden firs, which ran along the ridge like a battalion of spike-helmeted Prussian Guards. 'If we get caught out in those woods, we're in real trouble.'

And, for once, Matz did not object. The job of lookout at the point couldn't be left to one of the young soldiers. It was too important; the fate of the whole battle-group might well depend upon it. One minute later the Skoda's massive engine burst into life, emitting great clouds of blue smoke on the still morning air. The driver let out the clutch. They were on their way.

All morning they crawled at a snail's pace through snow-bound woods, their progress hindered by the snowstorm which had descended upon them just after they set out.

Visibility was virtually zero, and the lone Skoda toiling up the long slopes was blanketed time and time again in a swirling cocoon of white flakes. The crew could crouch behind the protection of the turret, but the lookouts had to brave the icy flakes, their faces crimson with cold beneath the masks, their eyes blinded more often than not by tears, body numb with freezing misery. Their only consolation was the fact that the terrible snowstorm would not encourage the Russians to hang about in the woods.

Just before midday, the snow started to let up and ahead Schulze, who was the lookout, could see the trees beginning to thin out. They had reached the edge of the wood. Somewhere beyond was the village of Neustedt – and the Popovs. He ordered the radio operator to contact One-Flipper and tell him the news, then commanding the driver to take the Skoda a little way off the trail and out of sight, he said to Matz, 'Come on, ape-turd, let's go and have a look-see at the place ourselves, before the big chief comes up. '

Five minutes later the two of them studied the scene, carefully concealed in a snow hollow just at the edge of the wood, the snowfield ahead of them a gleaming white in the winter sun so that Matz was forced to exclaim, 'Why, it's like a Christmas card, Schulze!'

'Yes, but there's not much peace on earth and goodwill to all men on this particular one,' Schulze growled. 'Look over there.' He indicated dark spots at regular intervals between themselves and the little town in the distance. 'Foxholes – Popov foxholes.'

Matz did not reply. Instead, he watched in silence as to the right of the Russian line an enemy multiple mortar fired and sent a batch of rockets howling towards the town, trailing fiery angry red flames behind them, to explode in a cloud of thick brown smoke to the right of the place's little church.

'Stalin organs, eh?' It was One-Flipper. Carefully he slid into the hole next to the two NCOs. 'Got the place nicely sewn up, haven't they?' he continued, quickly summing up the situation with his trained eye. 'Continuous line, rocket artillery and – yes, over there, next to that barn or whatever it is – a company of tanks.'

'Tough nut to crack, sir?' Matz enquired.

One-Flipper hesitated a moment before replying. 'Not really. Apart from the tanks, I'd estimate there is about a company and a half of infantry between us and the place – and, after all, we have got surprise on our side.'

'Easy enough to get in, in other words, sir,' Schulze said. 'But it might be a lot more difficult to get out again, if the Popovs re-form, or manage to bring up reinforcements.'

'Exactly.' One-Flipper's eyes swept the snowbound terrain, already searching for a spot where he could make his break-through. 'Speed is of the essence. We've got to get in there, get the papers and – '

'And the field-mattresses,' Matz prompted hastily. 'One woman's like any other when you haven't had any for a couple of million years.'

'Yes, and the field-mattresses,' One-Flipper agreed.

'But what about these fellers from the Hermann Goering Division, sir?' Schulze asked. 'Presumably it was their job to protect them. What if they won't play ball and give up the papers? Who knows what kind of orders Fat Hermann gave their commanders. Those fly-boys from the *Luftwaffe* are a funny lot.'

'We'll deal with that problem when we come to it. We've got to get in first,' One-Flipper said. 'Get ready to sound the charge, Schulze. We're going in for a surprise attack, eh!' In high good humour that his mission was apparently almost completed, he pressed a catch on that remarkable cane of his. A wicked-looking blade slid out of the end. Waving the cane around his head like a sabre, he chortled, 'To the attack, my brave boys! To the attack!'

Schulze got to his feet slowly and shook his head in mock sadness. 'I don't know,' he exclaimed, 'the officers we poor stubble-hoppers have got to put up with these days . . . I just don't know!'

One-Flipper laughed.

FIVE

'DRIVER – ADVANCE!' One-Flipper yelled over the intercom.

The Crocodile burst out of the trees in a shower of snow. All along the line of trees at the edge of the wood, the other vehicles of Battle-Group Flosse did the same.

'Co-ax, five hundred, fire!' One-Flipper commanded. 'Gunner target two o'clock – tanks, *fire*!'

In an instant, the turret was made with the chatter of the machine gun and the thump-thump of the cannon. Fumes blew back sharp and choking, sucked up towards the ventilator fans. One-Flipper pressed his forehead against the periscope pad.

The sudden fire from their rear had taken the Russians by surprise. Already one of their T-34s was burning fiercely and the crews were pelting back and forth across the snow, obviously not knowing whether to make a run for it or try to mount up and fight their tanks. 'Keep spraying them with the co-ax,' One-Flipper yelled. 'Don't give them a chance to organize!'

Now the armoured 'V' was careering madly across the bumpy snowfields that separated the force from Neustedt, throwing up huge wakes of flying snow. Russian fire pattered off the armoured sides, drumming on the metal like heavy tropical rain on a tin roof, but the Wotan men, carried away by the excitement of this wild charge, did not notice. The first Russians loomed up in their foxholes, faces crazed with fear, screaming unintelligibly. The Wotan showed no mercy. Tank after tank crashed into the holes, swirling round and round with flying tracks, until the foxholes gave way and were turned into horrible coffins filled with a bloody pulp which had once been a man.

Schulze's Skoda crashed through a barn, sending planks flying on all sides. A T-34 stood there broadside on, its driver fumbling furiously with his controls. Schulze's gunner didn't give him a chance. The 75mm roared. The solid white AP shell sped flatly across the intervening space. The T-34 was struck squarely between the deck and turret. The ten-ton turret sailed lazily into the air, while below the T-34 started to burn immediately.

The Skoda rolled on, lead howling harmlessly off its metal sides. It began to work its way down a line of trees which masked Neustedt beyond. They were full of confused Russians who were going down like flies, victims of the Skoda's chattering machine gun. It smashed through some thick snow-heavy foliage. Before it there loomed a sudden bank. The driver could do nothing else but take it. Slowly the thirty-five-ton self-propelled gun edged its way upwards. It reached the top. Beyond lay Neustedt. It poised there for a moment, hull raised high in the air, with Schulze praying that there was no Ivan anti-tank gun anywhere in the near vicinity; with their virtually unarmoured bottom in the air they were sitting ducks. But the danger came from elsewhere. Suddenly the panic-stricken voice of the driver came through the intercom, 'I can't hold it . . . The Skoda's slipping!'

Schulze flung a wild glance over the high side. The bank was beginning to break away. The nearside track started to race impotently. 'In God's name, *hold her*!' Schulze bellowed.

But that wasn't to be. The track lost traction completely. In a crazy rush, the Skoda slid down the bank, struck some hidden obstacle and overturned with a great crash that sent Schulze flying out of the open turret, his head ringing furiously, crazy red stars exploding in front of his eyes.

It was the chance the survivors of the Russian positions among the trees had been waiting for. Like a pack of hungry wolves sensing a fat prey they descended upon the Germans lying in and around the wrecked vehicle.

Schulze somehow got to his knees and pressed the trigger of his machine pistol, swinging his aching body from left to right. The running Ivans went down screaming piteously, as if swatted aside by a gigantic hand. But still more kept coming. Behind him the other shaken crew members were beginning to clamber out of the wreckage and grab for their weapons. Schulze knew he must cover them. He fired another burst and then the Schmeisser jammed. The Russians streamed forward, yelling that blood-curdling '*urrah!*' of theirs.

Schulze staggered to his feet, holding his Schmeisser like a bat. A Russian thrust at him with his bayonet. Schulze parried it with his weapon. Next instant he swung the Schmeisser back over his shoulder and struck the Russian a tremendous blow across the face. He went reeling back, spitting out teeth from a bloody hole, his face an unrecognizable crimson mess.

And then the Russians were all over the handful of Wotan men and Schulze felt himself go down, pulled to the ground by two slant-eyed stinking Siberian riflemen, lashing out with his great steel-shod dice-beakers at others trying to grab his feet, cursing and bellowing like some massive beast.

One-Flipper did not hesitate when he saw the overturned Skoda and the furious mêlée taking place in the snow. 'Cinders,' he commanded, 'now you're really going to have to show what a marksman you are . . . You've got to scare those Popovs away from that Skoda and not harm our own boys. Got it?'

'Got it,' Cinders answered in that typical grumpy manner of his.

'All right, driver, give gas! Let's go!'

The Crocodile started to waddle towards the overturned tank, the red indicator lamp of the flame-thrower glowing on the wall, testifying to the fact that Cinders was already prepared for action. Now they were some two hundred metres away from the confused scene around the Skoda, the Wotan men buried in a mass of grey-coated Russians. One-Flipper knew he couldn't wait any longer if he were going to save Schulze and his crew. 'The ones to the right in the trees, Cinders,' he ordered. 'Flame them. It might scare the other bastards off. *Flame!*'

One-Flipper said a silent prayer that the grumpy old gunner would be accurate as ever and not flame their own people and pressed his forehead against the rubber pad of the periscope.

Cinders fired. There was a great hiss, an abrupt sucking intake of air, and that terrifying rod of flame shot forward, scorching and searing all in its path. The fire crashed into the first tree, swung round it, sending scarred branches raining down, hit the next one and then ran down the whole line of terrified Russians crouching there.

The heat was terrific. Schulze, buried beneath a pile of Russians who were no longer attempting to take his life, could feel the breath being dragged from his lungs. He gasped frantically, his nostrils suddenly assailed by the sweet ghastly stench of burning flesh. Somewhere to his right the flame-thrower roared again like some primeval monster sensing blood. He felt himself break out in a thick sweat. He wanted to scream. The heat was unbearable. Unseen by Schulze, hidden by the bodies, a whole line of Russians was sumberged by that terrible, all-consuming flame, the roaring air full of their screams and eerie inhuman cries for help, as they were devoured by those scarlet maws. And then it was over, and when Schulze emerged from his hiding place he was confronted by a stark line of pygmies, frozen into rigid death, their charred claws, through which the bones gleamed a pearly-white, reaching up to an unfeeling sky, as if pleading for the mercy which never came.

One minute later, the Crocodile had crunched its way over the blackened shrunken bodies and Schulze, Matz and three other survivors of the Skoda crew were hauled aboard. The advance continued. But now the Russians had had enough. They were fleeing the field everywhere, throwing away their weapons in their haste to escape that terrible mobile flame-thrower.

The Crocodile took the lead. They could see Neustedt

quite clearly now, with the houses minus their roofs everywhere and the great gaps made by the Russian shells hastily filled in with lumber and pieces of furniture. A small camouflaged car raced across their front. The second-gunner pressed the trigger of his machine gun. Its windscreen vanished in a crazy jigsaw of broken glass. The blinded driver lost control and smashed into the wall of a barn, the little car's bonnet crumpling like a banada skin. The driver swung round the wrecked Russian car, which was already beginning to burn furiously, the dead driver slumped over the wheel, and there in front of them was the first barricade.

'Hold your fire, gunner!' One-Flipper bellowed hastily. He had recognized the shape of the helmets of the men holding it. They were German. They had done it. They had broken through to Neustedt. A few seconds later they were surrounded by cheering, laughing *Luftwaffe* men, who looked sorely in need of a good meal, slapping their rescuers, as they took Wotan to be, on the back, and crying, *'We never thought you could make it! Never thought it!'* Over and over again. Some of them were crying.

SIX

'What a heap!' Schulze exclaimed as he and Matz left the excited throng of soldiers surrounding the tanks. 'Have you ever seen so much tin, tinsel and scrambled egg in one mob? Every man-jack of them looks like a shitting full general!'

Matz nodded. The men of the Hermann Goering Division were worn, pale and emaciated, but their skinny chests were covered with an amazing variety of decorations and insignia. 'They're all former air-crew, Schulzi. Pilots without planes and the like – that's why Fat Hermann turned them all into infantry.'

'No wonder *they* got themselves in such a mess, trapped up here in this frozen arsehole of the world.' The word 'trapped' seemed to remind the big NCO of the little clandestine mission One-Flipper had given him before he had gone off to report to the Hermann Goering's company commander. 'Come on, Matzi,' he commanded, 'let's see if we can find the field-mattresses and Fat Hermann's papers.'

Matz's bruised, unshaven face lit up and he grabbed the front of his ragged, oily trousers eagerly. 'Now yer talking my language, man,' he exclaimed.

Together they strolled through the shell-shattered streets, apparently casually, stopping to look at the ruined little houses to which the war had brought a sudden intrusion into their private intimacy, nodding at the few shabby, starving civilians who scuttled by, looking at the two SS men as if they were visitors from another planet, and pausing to chat with the half-starved *Luftwaffe* soldiers on duty at every corner. The village school was occupied by soldiers. Civilians huddled in the ruined church. And the *Rathaus*[1] was filled to overflowing with wounded men, lying moaning or strangely silent in lice-ridden straw that stank of urine, ether and human misery. In the end it was Matz who discovered the field-mattresses' whereabouts.

Stopping dramatically and barring Schulze's progress with an outflung arm, he raised his nose to the air and sniffed delicately as if savouring some rare, delicious odour.

'What is it, you turd?' Schulze demanded. 'Got yer hooter too close to your fart-cannon or something?'

'Must you be so crude, you naughty fellow?' Matz simpered with fake daintiness. 'Can't you smell it?'

'Smell what?'

'The most delectable smell known to man.'

'Eh!'

'*GASH!*' Matz cried with delight. 'And it's coming from over there.'

[1] Town-hall.

Schulze followed the direction of his outstretched finger. The little corporal was pointing at Neustedt's former Party headquarters, its brick front now pocked with a myriad bullet holes, which contrasted strongly with the pair of female underpants hanging from the line attached to the building. He whistled softly at the sight. The massive red flannel knickers hung from the line, frozen stiff and extended at the legs, so that they looked like a suspended giant.

Matz breathed out in awe. 'Great God and all his triangles, Schulze. You would have to have something in yer britches to satisfy whatever fits into them bacon-bags.'

'And what is that supposed to mean, Corporal?' a deep resonant voice demanded imperiously.

Surprised, they both swung round to face the biggest woman that either of them had ever seen. She was a head taller than Schulze, her grey hair cropped as short as that of any SS recruit in basic training, with a definite suspicion of a black moustache beneath her great beak of a nose, from which at that particular moment a large dewdrop hung.

Matz's mouth dropped open stupidly and instinctively he grabbed Schulze's arm, as if for protection.

'Are you talking about my – er – underthings?' the gimlet-eyed woman barked.

Confused and not a little frightened by the field-mattress's formidable appearance, Schulze could do nothing but shake his head.

'Well, what are you prowling around here for, eh? After the skirts, I'll be bound, what?' She spread her legs that reminded Schulze of the piano legs of his youth, thrust her hands on her broad hips and puffed out her bosom so that it took on the appearance of a small barrage balloon, as if she were preparing herself to deny them entry physically.

Schulze swallowed hard and took in her insignia, which made her out to be a senior sergeant. 'Sorry for that remark, comrade,' he said humbly. 'Didn't realize that those bac – er – garments belonged to another NCO.'

The remark had its effect. The hardness had gone out of the giant woman's voice when she spoke again. 'Everyone can make an honest mistake, comrade. But you must be more careful in the future.'

'I will, I will,' Schulze answered hastily.

'We heard that you and your – er – ladies,' Matz began.

'Female soldiers,' the woman interrupted him sternly. 'We might well be weak women in body, but all the same we are soldiers of the Reich.'

'Of course,' Matz agreed hastily, his head about level with that tremendous bosom, telling himself he wouldn't like to meet this particular 'weak woman' on a dark night alone. 'But anyway, comrade, we heard that you are the ones who have the honour of caring for the papers of the Reich Marshal himself.' He smiled winningly up at her.

She frowned. 'Have you never heard the words "state secret", comrade?' she said harshly.

'Yes, but – '

'There are no buts about it, comrade. Schnapps is schnapps and duty is duty. Now I must be gone. I have work to do, if you two comrades obviously haven't.' And with that she brushed by them, almost poking out Matz's eyes with that formidable bosom of hers and leaving Schulze staring in dismay at her massive grey-clad back.

One-Flipper fared little better in his efforts with the Goering Papers. The captain in charge of the Hermann Goering troops defending the village was a tall, worried, skinny officer, whose thin chest was covered with the honours of six years of war. Later, One-Flipper was to learn he was a former Stuka pilot who had been grounded through lack of aircraft and thus come to the infantry. Now he felt he had made some bad mistakes in his first ground mission. 'Quite frankly, Lieutenant,' he said, wiping his hand across his thinning hair, 'I made a complete balls-up of my assignment. Lost half a company on the first day and managed to get the rest surrounded here, complete with fifty gun-girls under that battle-axe Sergeant Irmtraut Bengel. God in heaven, have you seen her?' he groaned. 'She'd frighten away the most hairy-assed old soldier you've ever seen – even if he had a fifty-year-old horn on! But that's not the worst – I've got the whole of Reich Marshal Goering's private papers in my charge too. If I lose those, I might as well blow a bullet through my brains *now*!'

'That's why we're here, Captain Mueller.' One-Flipper seized the chance offered him by the *Luftwaffe* man's remark. 'To get you, the gun-girls and the papers out before the Ivans attack again. It's vital that they don't get their dirty paws on them, isn't it?' He looked hopefully at the other man, who was examining the white dust from the flaking ceiling which lay on his hand, after smoothing his hair, as if he felt he was suffering from dandruff now too.

'But you're from the SS, Lieutenant. And with all due respect and gratitude for having broken through to us, I can't put vital *Luftwaffe* documents in the hands of an SS officer.'

'We are both German,' One-Flipper reminded him softly.

'Agreed. And between us pastor's daughters, Lieutenant, at this moment, I'm prepared to put my command, myself, the gun-girls and those damned papers right under your orders. For the rest of the war if needs be. I'm a mechanic, not a soldier.' He frowned. 'But there is always Fat Hermann. I need an order from him before I can let you take charge of them for whatever happens next.'

'You mean the break-out?'

'Exactly.'

'But how can you get an order from him?' One-Flipper objected, taking a chance that no radio contact existed between the trapped Hermann Goering company and the outside world. 'You've got no communications with the rear.'

'Agreed. I know I sound foolish, ungrateful and stubborn, Lieutenant, but that – ' He stopped suddenly and cocked his head to one side.

'What is it?'

'Can't you hear?'

'No.'

'Sounds like an Ivan sewing-machine to me,' the captain said and reached for his helmet, adorned with the eagle-in-flight of the *Luftwaffe*. 'Come on, let's see.'

High in the grey snow-sky to the east, an exceedingly slow biplane was banking, seemingly oblivious to the tracer zipping up angrily in its direction, as the *Luftwaffe* soldiers knelt in the streets and fired furiously at the intruder.

'Thought so, sewing-machine. *Rata recce* plane, Lieutenant.'

One-Flipper could understand why the biplane got its name. Its single radial engine did sound like the noise made by some ancient treadle sewing-machine.

For what seemed an age, the biplane flew back and forth unhampered by the wild erratic fire of the men in the streets, then it slowly swung round and headed straight for the east, obviously satisfied that it had obtained the information it desired.

'Watch in the bucket, a light VD in the heart,' the captain said, using the old soldier's phrase to express despondency.

One-Flipper nodded gloomily and said, ''Fraid you're right, Captain. Recce flight to see what we've got on the ground down here. They will have obviously spotted my tin cans. My troopers didn't have time to hide them.'

'Yes, I'm afraid my people did hold them up. What now?'

One-Flipper stared thoughtfully at the grey mass of clouds building up to the east. 'I'm no prophet, Captain, but I'll make this prediction. If the snowstorm doesn't get here first, the Ivans will.' He touched his cane to his peaked cap with the tarnished silver of the death's-head badge. 'Now, if you will excuse me, I must see to my command . . .'

'And the break-out?' the *Luftwaffe* officer asked.

But One-Flipper was already gone, striding down the street as if he were in a great hurry.

SEVEN

The wind was rising by the second. It howled and whirled around the little half-timbered farm, raising little dancing flurries of snow, shaking the windows, rattling the ancient loose doors.

The tall thin officer in the field-grey of the German Army, who looked every inch the Prussian general he had once been in another life although now he wore neither decorations nor badges of rank, frowned, as if by doing so he could stop the noise. Ivan Davidovitch, small, ugly and with clever eyes behind the pince-nez he affected in imitation of his chief, Beria, grinned. General von Seydlitz was still every inch the Prussian aristocrat and officer. Nothing must interfere with his deliberations, not even the wind. He waited.

Outside he could see the squat figures of the Russian tank crews crouched in the cold, eating their *kavka* as it was, whereas the Germans of the Seydlitz Army had erected neat little shelters of whatever materials they had been able to find in the village and were busy warming theirs on little improvised stoves. He shook his head in unconscious imitation of his grandfather, the old rabbi. The Russians expected to die soon; why, therefore, go to the bother of making fires to warm what might be their last meal? What did it matter? The Germans were different; they would be working and planning until the very second when a bullet blasted their brains out.

'What do you think – er – comrade?' the general asked, suddenly swinging round to face the little Jew from the Secret Police, staring down at him from his commanding height.

Davidovitch shrugged. 'With permission, General,' he answered in his accented but fluent German, '*I* do not think on military matters. *You* do.'

Seydlitz groaned.

Davidovitch grinned. 'An unusual situation, General, eh – a Russian Jew and a German officer working together. But if I may be allowed to offer you some advice?'

'Please.'

'It has always been my experience while I've worked for Comrade Beria that action is good, inaction is bad.'

'I see. Thank you. In other words, you think I should attack the damned place, in spite of the kind of weather we're soon going to get out there?'

'I didn't say that,' Davidovitch answered, for he was a careful man who had survived for so long in the NKVD because he had been so careful. 'I just gave you the benefit of my experience.'

Von Seydlitz, his lean face grey and worn, stared out of the window of his farmhouse HQ for a moment, asking himself why the devil he had ever got himself involved in this damned business. The Russians couldn't be trusted; they never gave a clear statement like an honest German would and they always played the game with the cards held damned close to their chests. Right from the start he had not known where he stood for a single instant.

He looked at his 'political adviser', who in reality he knew was his guard, and said stonily, 'Well, to give you the benefit of my experience, comrade, everything is against attacking in the kind of weather we can expect soon. The tanks could get bogged down, the infantry held in place, even the artillery can freeze up in such temperatures.'

'All very true, General,' the little Jew answered, completely unimpressed. 'But who will take such things into account if the fascists escape from Neustedt? Can the weather pay the price of failure, eh?'

The threat was unmistakable and von Seydlitz was not such a hidebound Prussian that he did not realize what Davidovitch meant. The weather could not be made accountable – he could.

For what seemed a long time, there was silence inside the farmhouse. Outside the wind continued to rise, howling and tearing at the fabric of the building and whirling the snow in ever more frantic flurries, so that at times the stolid Russian tank crews eating their cold meal porridge were invisible to the watchers from within. Finally the little Jew broke the heavy silence. 'Comrade General,' he began.

The 'Comrade General' alerted the Prussian aristocrat. The 'Comrade' was a signal that Davidovitch was talking seriously. 'Yes,' he said.

'Our responsibility is to Comrade Beria; those tankers out there, for their part, are responsible to the Army and the Army to the *Stavka.*'

'I agree.'

'Well,' the little Jew said, obviously selecting his words with care, 'come what may, Comrade Beria never fails – never. Therefore those tankers out there should be used to ensure that Comrade Beria does not fail, regardless of whether the snowstorm comes or not. They are – how shall we phrase it – ' he smiled winningly at the tall skinny general, but his dark cunning eyes did not light up – 'expendable?'

Von Seydlitz waited.

'Let them bear the brunt of the attack on Neustedt. There is a battalion of T-34s out there and we know the Fritzes – excuse me, the Fascists – have perhaps some twenty armoured vehicles in Neustedt. Perhaps I agree with you that our men will not be able to break through under the present conditions, even if they are the superior force. The Fascists are brave, one must say that of them, eh?'

Von Seydlitz looked at the dirty wooden floor. His family had served Prussia and later Germany since the days of the Great Elector; he didn't like to be reminded of the fact that he was fighting against his own people. He said nothing.

'But even if they don't break through, they'll force the Fascists to do what they want to do as it is.'

'And that is?'

'To retreat with the papers of the fat pig Goering. Thinking that we have spent our powder for the time being, they will withdraw while there is a lull in the fighting. And this,

Comrade General, is where you come in. While the fighting is going on, perhaps even benefiting from the storm, if it comes, using it as cover – '

'I will make a left-hook around the place with my infantry,' von Seydlitz interrupted. He had not been a tactics teacher at the War Academy in his younger years for nothing, 'and then when they are out in the open . . .' He did not pursue the thought to its end. Instead he took out his watch and checked the time. It would be another four hours or so until darkness . . .

EIGHT

Now the sun, rime-ringed and a pale luminous yellow – a sure sign of snow – was beginning to set. It cast long shadows which raced like live things across the windswept snowfield to the village that, to a casual observer at least, seemed to be settling down for the night.

But that was not the case. Everywhere in the barns and the ruined houses, the Wotan troopers, the men of the Hermann Goering Division and the remaining peasants prepared for the withdrawal. The civilians fed their skinny nags and heavy ponderous oxen for a last time and harnessed them to the farm carts, already piled with their possessions. In the houses occupied by the Hermann Goering, the amateur soldiers oiled their weapons with the special winter grease to prevent the moving parts from freezing up in the arctic cold outside or helped to bed their wounded down in the Wotan's half-tracks, under whose engines already burned little fires so that their motors would start instantly. All was busy, anxious preparation for what must come soon. And outside in the gathering gloom the wind howled like a demented banshee.

In the kitchen of the little cottage which had been allotted to him as an HQ, One-Flipper ate slowly of his sandwich of dry black bread and sausage, watched by Schulze, who gnawed the end of the same sausage, and Matz, who observed both of them, hunger in his faded eyes; he had swapped his rations for a slug of home-made potato schnapps with a Hermann Goering soldier.

'What now, sir?' Schulze finally asked and, without looking round, tossed the hunk of sausage to Matz, who caught it neatly and began eating it greedily.

'Well, at the moment we can't get our hands on those Goering papers unless we fight those fly-boy soldiers,' One-Flipper answered.

'Not to be recommended under present circumstances?' Schulze asked, as if he had seriously considered the possibility. 'But all the same, sir, under the present set-up we're lumbered with those amateurs, the gun-girls and the civvies – a bunch of wet-tails who don't know one end of a rifle from the other, the lot of 'em.'

' 'Cept that big Irmtraut,' Matz said, his mouth full of sausage. 'One look from that field-mattress and a whole regiment of Popovs would piss themselves.'

They both nodded their agreement. Outside the wind howled frantically and the little house shook to its foundations, as if it might collapse at any moment.

'Well, we've got to accept the fact that we're taking the whole bunch with us,' One-Flipper continued after a moment. 'I'm not exactly a sister-of-mercy but we can't let the Popovs slaughter the civvies and those women soldiers.'

'Gash is gash,' Matz said apropos of nothing.

'Once we've reached our lines, we can see about getting our paws on those papers. So how are we going to organize them?' He answered his own question. 'The civvies go out first in their own trek. We'll give them a route, a few hours' start on our own convoy and a handful of those cardboard soldiers from the Hermann Goering as protection. We'll take out the rest, the wounded and the Hermann Goering fly-boys.'

'And the Goering papers, sir?' Schulze asked. '*Where* are they?'

'There are two possibilities to my way of thinking,' One-Flipper replied slowly. 'The Hermann Goering haven't much in the way of transport left. After all they were employed as infantry. But they have their CO's command car – that thing with all the radio aerials, so that it looks like a mobile Christmas tree – and the big truck the field-mattresses use. Both are soft-skinned and would go up like a lighter if a Russian shell came within sniffing distance of them; all the same Captain Mueller insists they should go out with the armoured convoy. More importantly Sergeant Irmtraut does too.'

'So you think they're in one of those two, the Goering documents, I mean, sir?' Matz queried, licking his greasy fingers and savouring the last of the sausage.

One-Flipper nodded.

'Should be easy enough to find out, sir,' Schulze said. 'Put some of our people in both of the vehicles to guard them.'

'No can do. Captain Mueller was adamant about that. That is why I suspect the documents are in one of those two cars. But never fear, Schulze, we'll find out in due course where they are. However, we must make sure that those two vehicles are not lost during the break-out. I want them boxed-in somewhere in the centre of the armoured convoy. You, Schulze, will be made responsible for seeing that nothing happens to Captain Mueller's car, and you, Matz, for Big Irmtraut's.'

Matz blanched. 'But why me, sir? What have I done to be lumbered with that piece of monstrous slit? I'm only little and I've got a peg-leg too.'

Schulze guffawed at the look of genuine alarm on his running-mate's face. 'And a little dingle-dong as well. Why don't you use yer peg-leg instead, ape-turd?'

'Schulze,' One-Flipper said, 'hold your tongue, you rogue, and listen. The civvies I want to move off as soon as it's sufficiently dark. We follow three hours later. It's going to be hell once the snowstorm hits us, but you Wotan stubble-hoppers are not made of sugar. You're used to it. The main thing is to keep the convoy closed up so that no one goes astray.'

'The boys won't let you down, sir,' Schulze said with conviction. 'But what about the Popovs, sir? What are they going to be doing while we're taking a nice little nocturnal sleigh-ride?'

'I think and hope that whatever counter-attack they might well be planning to put in on Neustedt at the moment will be delayed by the coming snow.' It was exactly at that moment that the first enemy mortar-shell tore the evening air apart with its terrifying howl and someone outside shouted urgently, 'Hit the dirt! *Incoming mail . . .*' and One-Flipper knew that his plan for a peaceful evacuation of Neustedt had failed. *Now he would have to make a fight for it!*

Three
Retreat from Neustedt

ONE

'C-rump!' Once again scarlet flame stabbed the whirling howling fog of the snowstorm. The T-34 reared up on its bogies and came to a dead stop, as if it had just run into a brick wall. Flames leapt up from its burning motor. The Russian tankers flung themselves out of the escape hatches and doubled for cover. They didn't get far. Instantly the machine gunners of the Hermann Goering covering the Skoda self-propelled gun which had knocked out now its fifth T-34 opened up. The Russians skidded to a stop, hands fanning the air wildly, and slumped down into the snow.

'T-34 from the right!' somebody screamed.

With a great heave of his shoulder, Schulze spun the 75mm gun round. Another T-34 had come roaring in from the snow-mist, its cannon spitting fire. An eighty-pound shell hissed just above the Skoda's open turret, sending it rocking from side to side, as if it had been caught in a great wind. Schulze did not let himself be distracted from his purpose. He waited one second more, until the Russian tank filled the whole horizon in front of him, then he pulled back the firing bar. The Skoda reared back like a horse being put to the saddle for the first time. Automatically Schulze blinked his eyes and opened his mouth so that the blast would not burst his eardrums. The great flame cleared to reveal the T-34 bowled completely over like an upturned turtle, its tracks still running.

'Number six!' Matz cried joyously. 'Christ on a crutch, Schulze, you've never been this good before with the old pea-shooter!'

'Can't miss the silly shits, they're so thick on the ground,' Schulze bellowed over the howl of the storm and wiping fresh snowflakes from his red streaming face, took aim again.

Fifty metres away, crouched on the turret of the Crocodile, together with Captain Mueller of the Hermann Goering, One-Flipper took in the scarlet flames that broke the grey wall of flying snow everywhere, and gave vent to the same awed sentiment. 'They're so thick on the ground, one can't miss, Captain.'

'My boys are loving it,' Mueller yelled back, hands cupped around his mouth, excited and happy in spite of his snow-laden uniform and his frozen face. 'God in heaven, we must have knocked out at least twenty of the Popovs! Their commander must be a complete idiot to keep on attacking like this in this kind of weather, with your people dug in a hull-down position.'

'Who knows?' One-Flipper cried back, the wind snatching the words from his mouth and slapping his uniform tightly against his lean body. He raised his one hand and peered through the flying white gloom at the luminous dial of his watch. It was nearly midnight. The civilian trek had been gone for nearly three hours now. They had had a good start and he was pretty sure that none of the T-34s attacking the village had been able to sneak round Neustedt and intercept them. 'All I know is we can't stick this out much longer. In the morning they'll bring up air. As soon as this storm blows over they'll be dropping the usual square eggs on us by the dozen.'

'That's true. What do you suggest?'

Another T-34 came charging out of the snow. Half a dozen 75mms and 105s ranged in on it at once. It reeled from side to side, as it was hit repeatedly, giving off the hollow sound of metal striking metal. Finally, its long over-hanging gun drooped to the ground and thick grey smoke started to pour from its turret. No one got out.

'We get out, as soon as we can. Break off the action and move out in sections.'

'I've heard it's tricky.' Mueller bellowed over the wind.

'If anyone panics and begins to run, all hell will be let loose. Everything has got to be disciplined and controlled.'

He clapped his hands around his mouth and yelled above the howl of the mortars, which were now beginning to bombard the shattered village, the obvious prelude to yet another suicidal charge on the part of the Russians. 'You take the van, Captain, I'll bring up the rear. Agreed?'

One-Flipper caught a swift glimpse of Mueller's face by the red glare of an exploding mortar bomb. It was greased as if with sweat and the eyes were wild, filled with a mixture of fear and excitement; Mueller was high on the excitement of danger. He sniffed and wondered whether he had any coke left; he'd need it tonight.

'Who shall I take in the van, Lieutenant?'

'The bulk of your own people, the wounded in my half-tracks, the field-mattresses and a couple of my SPs, commanded by Sergeant-Major Schulze and Matz to give you a bit of muscle. They're very experienced – ' He ducked again as a battery of Stalin Organs opened up to their right, the rockets screeching into the sky, dragging enormous trails of smoke and fiery sparks behind them. *One . . . two . . . three . . . four . . . five . . . six . . .* they came crashing down, shaking the forty-ton Crocodile violently, sending shrapnel hissing through the air terrifyingly and cutting down a whole line of Hermann Goering men who had not ducked quickly enough, turning their position into a blood-bath of torn, screaming, writhing dying and wounded men.

One-Flipper knew he couldn't waste any more time. In spite of the success of their defence, the fly-boys were taking too many casualties simply because they were inexperienced. 'Captain, you'd better start getting yourself organized. I'll have those two self-propelled guns withdrawn from my line. Place one behind your own command car in case you bump into anything nasty on the way out and the other behind the gun-girls – they're the most vulnerable of your force.'

Mueller crouched on the edge of the Crocodile's deck. 'And you?'

'Don't worry about me. I'll keep in radio contact with Sergeant-Major Schulze in the SP behind you. We'll find you. Now, with all due respect, make dust, Captain, while you've still got time. HERE THEY COME AGAIN . . .'

Now the sound of heavy firing behind them started to die away, muted by the howling storm that covered the decks of the vehicles, ankle-deep in soft snow, and made it a nerve-racking business for the drivers to keep in contact with the vehicle in front and at the same time to fight the slick, treacherous trail, which threatened to overturn them or throw them in the ditch at every fresh bend.

Schulze, his face hidden by the leather face-mask, strained his eyes trying to keep the faint tail-light of Captain Mueller's command car in view and wondered where all this was going to lead to. One-Flipper was a vet like himself and a cynic to boot; why would he go to such lengths to steal a bunch of papers for the *Reichsheini*? What did he mean by stating he had a wife in Neuengamme Concentration Camp? It wasn't exactly customary for a professional SS officer to have his slit in a concentration camp. What the hell had he, One-Flipper, done to have been given a mission like this?

Behind his mask, Schulze's brow creased in a frown. So many questions, with apparently no answers. Yet somehow he had confidence in One-Flipper. During the Popov attack on Neustedt he had shown that he knew how to handle men in battle and yet he was no death-or-glory boy, eager to throw his men's lives away for his own personal advancement, as so many young SS officers were. So far they hadn't lost a man. One-Flipper was sticking to his promise that he was not going to lead any Ascension-Day Commando. All the same, Schulze was uneasy. This wasn't the kind of combat he liked: where German fought German, men's lives were risked for political advantage, and women were involved. He frowned and wished suddenly it was all over and he could get what was left of the Wotan back to a normal combat outfit.

Thus the long night passed, with the drivers fighting the driving snow, grinding their way higher and higher into the forest, each man and woman wrapped in his own lonely freezing miserable cocoon of snow, wondering whether dawn would ever come again – or whether some evil fate had condemned them to this misery for all time.

But dawn did come and with it an end to the snow. Wearily Captain Mueller called a brief halt and posted guards, who dropped to the fresh gleaming new snow with stiff, wooden limbs to take up their positions while the women, under the eagle-eye of Big Irmtraut, disappeared into the cover of the snow-heavy firs to relieve themselves.

Matz plodded through the knee-deep snow and breaking his last cigarette in half, handed a piece to Schulze. 'Lung torpedo,' he grunted. Schulze grunted something and wordlessly they puffed out the rich blue smoke, savouring the only pleasure granted them this freezing wartime dawn in the middle of no-man's land. All around them the emaciated Hermann Goering soldiers stamped their feet and swung their arms across their chests in a vain attempt to get warm.

Captain Mueller, blue-lipped and as frozen as were his men, was just about to blow his whistle and order the men to mount up once more, when the scream came and a panic-stricken field-mattress came stumbling out of the trees, her hair streaming out behind her, her face contorted with fear, screaming, screaming and screaming, as if the devil himself were after her.

Instinctively Schulze dropped his precious cigarette stump and grabbed for his machine pistol. Next to him Matz did the same. Together they plodded heavily through the snow to where Mueller stood, facing the girl, pistol held in a nervous, frightened hand. 'What is it?' he cried, his voice shaky.

But all he could get out of the girl was a meaningless throaty gurgling, accompanied by a hectic wave of her hand in the direction from which she had just come running. In the end Big Irmtraut stepped forward and, drawing back her big hand, slapped the panic-stricken girl across the face. That shocked her into silence and Big Irmtraut said in that thick gruff masculine voice of hers, 'Now then, remember you're a soldier, too! What is it? Why are you carrying on like this?'

The girl, a pretty if insipid blonde whose skirt buttons, Matz noted, were undone, as if she had been surprised by whatever had thrown her into such terror in the act of relieving herself, sobbed and then gasped, 'Bodies, bodies . . . bodies everywhere out there!' And then she broke down altogether and fell sobbing on to the massive bosom of a surprised Big Irmtraut.

'Come on, Captain,' Schulze cried, reacting quicker than Mueller. 'Let's have a look-see. Matz, take over here! Get the gunners on to their pea-shooters. See those wet-tails from the Hermann Goering get the lead out of their butts. *Captain!*'

Together the two men plodded through the deep snow, while behind them the weary convoy was galvanized into action, weapons at the ready, their breath fogging the icy air in grey clouds. Automatically Schulze searched for the well-known tread of a Russian Army boot, cleated instead of nailed as was the case with the *Wehrmacht* footwear. But there were none. Whoever might have been there during the night, all traces of their passing had been obliterated by the snowstorm. They went by the spot where the field-mattresses had relieved themselves, the snow stained a bright yellow everywhere, pushed on, forcing their way through some firs, and stopped.

A body lay there, propped against the severed stump of a tree, as if placed there deliberately. The face was that of a typical East Prussian farmer, dark and muscular and with that expression of clever stubbornness and surface servility, common to their faces. Now his upper plate hung from his open mouth to give a mocking aspect to it, as if to say 'you won't catch me out'. But they had. His ribs were shattered, his lungs visible through red and white-flecked gory torn flesh.

Captain Mueller fought down the bitter green bile that had risen sickeningly into his throat and said thickly: 'It's one of the peasants –' he swallowed again – 'the peasants from the convoy.'

'Come on,' Schulze snapped, a dreadful suspicion filling his mind, 'up round the bend!'

As quickly as they could, their weapons gripped at the ready, the two men waded through the knee-high snow. They swung round the bend – and stopped dead.

It was the convoy all right, just as Schulze had suspected. Dead horses and oxen lay everywhere, their legs already stretched out and rigid in that icy cold so that with their bloated stomachs they looked like tethered barrage balloons. But it wasn't the dead animals which caught their shocked attention; it was the slaughtered men, women and children.

They lay everywhere in the violent and extravagant postures of the sudden-dead, caught completely by surprise by whoever had massacred them, their pathetic possessions littering the trail.

'Oh, my God!' Captain Mueller exclaimed in a stifled voice. 'The Popovs did this. But they're civvies!' He looked down at a dead girl, her face ripped off by machine-gun fire but still clutching an old doll in her skinny arms. 'They were unarmed.'

Schulze said nothing. Sombrely he stepped over the dead body of an old woman, with her skirts thrown up and her legs apart to reveal her faded patched bloomers in the kind of obscene invitation she had never known in life. He raked around in the little depression in the snow he had spotted there. A handful of gleaming empty cartridge cases appeared. He looked at the base of one of them, slowly deciphering the Cyrillic lettering: 'MOSKVA'. 'Moscow,' he raised his voice. 'Yes, the bastards were Russian all . . .' He stopped short, his attention suddenly caught by the imprint of a boot. It was nailed in the German fashion and not cleated. 'The Seydlitz Army,' he whispered.

'What did you say?' Mueller said, crossing to him, taking care to avoid the dead, looking like an awkward child playing hop-scotch in his attempt not to step on them.

'Captain,' Schulze said urgently, guessing now what had happened. 'I haven't got much time to tell you the facts of life at this moment, but I'll tell you this. They tried to pin us down at Neustedt, throwing away their tanks like that, in order to outflank us. They knew we'd pull back and they were waiting for us. Only in the darkness and that storm they made a mistake. They mistook those poor shits of civvies for us.'

'You mean they're up ahead of us somewhere?'

'I mean exactly that,' Schulze said grimly, tossing away the cartridge case and staring at the dead body of a peasant, from whose rucksack there protruded a pair of silver candlesticks, as if he had thought he had been on his way to some East Prussian party, complete with schnapps and beer and Konigsberg meatballs in thick gravy to be eaten by candlelight, instead of sudden death.

Captain Mueller looked around at the silent snow-heavy firs, as if he had expected the Russians to start coming out firing at any moment. 'But what are we going to do, Sergeant-Major?'

'First I'm going to contact Lieutenant Flosse on the radio and tell him what has happened up here. Then we'll take it from there.' Leaving Mueller standing, there, he ran awkwardly back to the rest of the convoy, ignoring the questions of the freezing soldiers and the anxious frightened looks of the women, to clamber on to the Skoda.

By the time Mueller came back, he had received his orders and had transmitted them under his voice to Matz, who had blanched but said nothing.

'Well?' Mueller demanded, staring up at the big SS man standing in the turret above him.

'Lieutenant Flosse is on his way with the rest of Wotan, sir. They have successfully broken off the action with the Popovs.'

'Thank God for that.' Mueller sighed with relief, knowing that he was completely out of his depth now and that if he was ever going to get his own men back to the German lines, he would need all the help he could get from the SS. 'And what did your officer say we should do, Schulze?'

Schulze hesitated an instant. 'He said, sir, we should continue as we are.'

Mueller looked shocked. 'But if they're out there . . .' His voice trailed away, as if he dare not think that terrible thought to an end.

Schulze shrugged carelessly. 'Those were the orders I was supposed to pass on to you, sir.' And without waiting for any further reaction from Mueller, he bent inside the turret and bellowed, 'All right, plush-ears, get this tin-can rolling again. *Carbide!*'

TWO

An uneasy stillness like a premonition of impending danger hung over the snowy landscape, so thick, Schulze told himself, that you could cut it with a knife. To another eye, the snow-heavy trees sparkling in the thin hard light of the winter morning sun, the clean invigorating air, the immense blue wash of the sky, might have seemed beautiful; a scene of peace and winter happiness as portrayed by some romantic early-nineteenth-century painter. But not to Schulze. He was an old hand. He could smell the danger that was waiting for them as the convoy crawled towards the abandoned farmhouse.

At that distance, it seemed a very substantial place for a traditional impoverished East Prussia, with heavy-block stone walls and fine slate room, with what looked like large stone-walled animal-pens on both sides. It had been the pens that had convinced Captain Mueller, who had still not overcome his fears of an ambush, that it would be an ideal place for the van to wait until One-Flipper caught up with them.

'We can get the vehicles tucked away safely inside those walls, Schulze,' he had announced, lowering his binoculars after surveying the place thoroughly. 'And no one will be the wiser we're there.'

Schulze had not objected, thinking of what One-Flipper had ordered him to do over the radio. He didn't say to the inexperienced fly-boy, 'Look, Captain, with not a building within kilometres of here, don't you think that is exactly where the enemy will think that a bunch of inexperienced wet-tails with the egg-shell still behind their spoons will head for?' Instead he had shrugged and said, 'As the Captain commands.'

Keeping his eye on Mueller's command car, he directed the Skoda expertly into the narrow confines of the animal pen, to the right of the big, empty and somehow sinister farmhouse. But, when a few moments later he followed Captain Mueller on his inspection of the place, everything seemed very normal. As they walked through the empty rooms, the only thing that seemed strange about the farmhouse was that it was not occupied. Everything was in place, even to the dark, air-cooled hams and sides of bacon hanging from the beams, which Schulze's expert eye had already reserved for Wotan's NCO Corps – namely himself and Matz.

Captain Mueller seemed satisfied too. Completing his inspection, he gave his orders. Sentries would be posted in the upper floor to watch for Lieutenant Flosse's arrival. Meanwhile the field-mattresses could rest and then help to cook whatever they could find in the kitchen, which boasted a large pump that had not frozen up. Mueller studied his map for a few moments to work out their position, then passed on the co-ordinates to a waiting Schulze. 'See that your radio operator gets those to Lieutenant Flosse immediately, Sergeant-Major, and then consider yourself off-duty for a while.' He smiled for the first time since they had left Neustedt. 'Me, I'm going to get these dice-beakers off. It's three days since I last saw my feet. God, how they smell . . .

I think one can safely say that we're nearly home and dry now, Sergeant Schulze, eh?'

But all the *Luftwaffe* captain received in reply from Schulze was a morose, non-committal grunt.

General von Seydlitz lowered his glasses. 'Very amateurish,' he said severely, as if he were some pre-war umpire at a manoeuvre, criticizing an inefficient young officer. 'The damn fool has got what bit of armour he possesses tucked away in that cattle pen, so that he has no possible chance of monoeuvring them.' He shook his head. 'Tut-tut, it is really not good enough.'

Davidovitch, crouched in the trees next to the German, smiled softly to himself and concentrated on surveying the farmhouse down below with his own binoculars. There really was something of a picnic atmosphere to the whole scene. Women were walking around in twos combing their hair as they strolled, while soldiers, weapons slung carelessly over their shoulders, drank out of their canteens or lounged in doorways looking at the women. And the General was right about the enemy's vehicles. They were neatly lined up in the two pens, both SP guns boxed in by the soft-skinned vehicles, as if they were awaiting inspection. When the shit hit the fan, those two Skodas wouldn't have a chance in hell of getting into action.

He lowered his glasses and turned to the General, whose long, lean, intellectual face reflected his disgust at what he saw below. 'Well, General?' he asked.

'Most disgusting,' von Seydlitz said to himself. 'One wonders what has become of the German Officer Corps these last years.'

Davidovitch was tempted to tell him, but decided against it. 'The plan?' he persisted. 'What now?'

'Oh, the plan,' von Seydlitz echoed. 'Really, a good twelve-year man[1] and not a full general with general staff

[1] In the pre-war German Army a regular NCO served for 12 years.

training could deal with this minor tactical problem quite easily. Seal the house off from the vehicles.'

'Yes, those vehicles must not be damaged on account of the Goering documents,' Davidovitch agreed hastily.

'Make a show of strength – a minor skirmish on both flanks should suffice. Follow that up by a brief mortar stonk and then ask for their surrender. A very routine exercise, I can assure you.' He glanced at his watch, a present from his father the day he had graduated from the Academy, and bit his bottom lip suddenly, as if he had recalled abruptly that the 'enemy' he was about to attack was of his own blood. 'Two hours I'd give them, two hours at the most.'

Captain Mueller sprawled out on the bed, wriggling his toes happily between taking delighted bits of the piece of air-cured bacon that the NCO Corps of SS Assault Regiment Wotan, in the person of Corporal Matz, had kindly offered him. 'This is the life,' he chortled and raised his piece of bacon as if to toast the yellowing picture of a moustached farmer and his big-bosomed wife on the wall next to the wooden crucifix. 'Hayseed, the Greater German *Luftwaffe* salutes and thanks you!'

Schulze grinned. Mueller was not a bad bastard. He was a typical smooth-head, red, fly-boy, more at home in bars surrounded by pretty, admiring girls, boasting of his exploits in the 'wild blue yonder' than in the rough-and-ready world of the front-swine. He took another bite of the excellent smoked black sausage and wondered when the balloon would go up. One-Flipper had told him over the radio to expect trouble soon, but had ordered him not to warn the Fly-Boy; he might well give the game away.

'Do you know in the old days, Schulze and Matz,' Mueller continued, 'we'd take off in the morning on a dive-bombing mission, knock the crap out of some Tommy convoy or other, get back for lunch to the mess – in those days there was always champagne in the mess after a mission – and be down in the local houses-of-joy, as they are so quaintly described, by – '

The single shot shattered the glass of the window opposite into a glittering spider-web with startling suddenness.

'*What* – ' Mueller's cry was interrupted by the chatter of a machine gun. On the wall the crucifix leapt abruptly and came tumbling down, Christ in splinters.

'*Sound the alarm!*' Schulze bellowed frantically above the rattle of small-arms fire which had broken out everywhere outside. '*Sound the shitting alarm!* Captain – ' He stopped short. The top of Captain Mueller's head had vanished. Thick scarlet blood was streaming down his abruptly ashen face.

'In those days there was always champagne . . .' The whispered words seemed to come from another world. Then the hand holding the bacon dropped to the bed. Captain Mueller was dead . . .

THREE

One-Flipper's boots made a sucking sound in the soft snow and he could feel his loosened helmet straps flapping against his skinny cheeks. But he was not worried by the noise he made. There was enough noise coming from below to cover any he made.

He sniffed and watched the white-camouflaged figures of the attackers crawl ever closer to the besieged farmhouse, firing controlled bursts as they moved forward, the mortar barrage which covered their approach flinging up great spurts of white that temporarily hid the house from sight. They were obviously veterans, élite troops, whose commander was not going to waste them in the usual massed Russian tactics, when the charging Ivan infantry was slaughtered by the hundred.

In spite of the seriousness of the Hermann Goering's position, he was forced to smile. If the attackers were veterans, the defenders really were the rankest of amateurs.

They had allowed themselves to be cut off from their vehicles and now they were caught with their skivvies down around their ankles, firing back from loop-holes made in the hastily piled up furniture at the windows, as if this were some pre-war American wild-west film and not the real thing where blood wasn't ketchup, but blood! He shook his head. 'Poor fly-boys,' he said to himself. 'Your eagles certainly have come down to earth with a nasty crash.'

Then he concentrated on the task at hand. The attackers had extended their flanks so that they had the house surrounded on three sides. Not that the escape route they had left open meant very much; the Hermann Goering men were effectively cut off from their vehicles and without them and burdened by the field-mattresses, they didn't stand a chance in hell of escaping. To the right of the house, the Russians had a battery of mortars, probably 47mms, dug in in a copse of trees with which they were covering the infantry's advance. They would present no problem, unless they managed to land a lucky shot into the open deck of a half-track or open turret of a self-propelled.

However in the end, although the Russian infantry outnumbered his own force by at least ten to one, it was armoured and he did have surprise on his side. He eyed the scene a little while longer and then made his decisions. He'd outflank them and roll them up from both sides. This time there could be no more mistakes. The German lines were only five or so kilometres away. When he reached them, he wanted to be in possession of the Goering Papers. Time was running out fast and *Irma* had to live.

The slug that howled off the plaster just above his head, coming from a direction from which they had taken no fire up to now, alerted Schulze to the new danger. Shaking the dust from his helmeted head like a bull trying to drive off some importuning flies in summer, he roared, 'Matz, after me!'

Matz dropped his machine pistol and swung round, his face streaked with sweat and powder burns. 'What?'

'You heard, plush-ears! After me!'

'Why?' Matz protested. 'It's dangerous out there. There's iron in the air.'

'And my dice-beaker will be up your arse-hole in half a second if you don't follow me. The slant-eyed shits are down in the outer pen. They could get the papers, if they're in the Captain's car or that of the gun-girls.'

'Holy strawstack, of course, you're right!'

'Of course I'm right. I always am . . . Come on, don't stand there like a fart in a trance.'

Together they clattered down the stone-flagged hall, ignoring the slugs whining off the walls everywhere. They flung open the door of the kitchen. There were field-mattresses spread out everywhere on the floor, hands held over their ears, eyes wild with fear, as bursts of machine-gun fire ripped through the air at waist-height, sawing through the big wooden farmhouse table, sending the pots and pans singing, shattering plate after plate in the big dresser.

Schulze caught a white glimpse of Big Irmtraut's massive thighs as she closed her legs rapidly and cried, 'What now, Sergeant-Major?'

'Tell your little ladies to keep their knees together, Irmtraut!' Schulze gasped. 'The Popovs are outside in the pens!'

'The Russians!' the cries of alarm went up on all sides. 'Oh, the beasts, they'll rape us!'

'Nonsense!' Big Irmtraut bellowed, rising to her feet and seizing the rolling-pin that a burst of fire had knocked to the floor, held it above her head in a hand like a ham. 'I'll soon settle their hash. Come on, you weak-kneed cowards. Don't let a weak little woman do your work for you.' She flung open the door, ignoring the bullets which were everywhere, and rushed into the pen, brandishing her rolling-pin.

A group of white-clad men rushed from behind the Skoda. Schulze and Matz fired as one. They slithered to a stop, legs giving weakly beneath them like those of a new-born foal. Another group came from the side of the command-car. Big Irmtraut's rolling-pin flew through the air and the first man hit the ground as if pole-axed. Big Irmtraut did not hesitate for one minute. She dived forward and took the other two down under the impact of that massive body. Immediately she started to pound them with her fists, and at the same time sank her teeth into the upper leg of the bigger of the two, who started to curse fluently in German.

But Schulze and Matz had no time for the field-mattress. There were infiltrators everywhere in the courtyard. Gasping furiously, they dodged from vehicle to vehicle, firing a quick burst, ducking the bullets directed at them, spurting forward over the bodies writhing in the suddenly blood-red snow, working their way to the gate which had been destroyed by the enemy mortar barrage.

A whole group of the enemy was rushing in in a closed body, obviously convinced that they could be careless now that the pen had been infiltrated by their own comrades. They were sorely mistaken. Standing crouched, legs apart like western gun-slingers, the two Wotan men fired burst after burst at the attackers. Faces set in hard relentless purpose, they poured a hail of slugs at the soldiers rushing towards them, turning them into a wall of kicking, writhing, dying men and then there were no more left of them.

It was only then that they remembered Big Irmtraut and her assailants. But their assistance was no longer needed. They found her squatting on top of the last survivor, the blood streaming from his nostrils indicating that he had suffered a severe concussion, frantically tugging at her skirt which had ridden up her massive thighs to reveal a pair of red flannel knickers and pink suspender straps. She blushed when she saw them and said severely, 'One would think you would have the common decency to avert your eyes while a lady adjusts her dress!'

Schulze's mouth dropped open stupidly, and Matz crossed himself reverently as if in the presence of the holiest of the holies, muttering, 'Kiss me, Mother, for I am to be Queen of the May . . .'

One-Flipper was grateful for the obscene thump of the

mortars and the great tearing whoosh of the Stalin Organs, as the Crocodile started to edge its way down the slope towards the unsuspecting Russian gunners. Not only was their own approach covered by their noise, but it would also prevent the attacking infantry hearing the rattle of his armour spreading out on both flanks in two great arcs.

'Two hundred metres to go,' he whispered through the mike to Cinders tensed below, as if the enemy might be able to hear them.

'Two hundred,' Cinders echoed.

To their front, the mortars continued their low and hideous moan, their crews going through the routine actions, bomb down the tube, ears covered instantly, faces turned away from the blast, crump, and the same procedure all over again. They crept ever closer. One-Flipper could see each man quite clearly in spite of the white camouflaged capes they wore. They wouldn't know what hit them. 'One hundred and fifty,' he whispered into the mike.

'One hundred and fifty it is,' Cinders replied obediently, presumably adjusting the range accordingly.

Then it happened. One of the sweating mortar crews turned, perhaps to check the ammunition piled in the snow to the rear of the tubes. The look of hectic action on his face changed to one of surprise, then fear. He opened his mouth to cry out. One-Flipper didn't give him a chance. '*FIRE!*' he bellowed.

There was that well-remembered hiss. A sound like leather being stropped. The fuel shot out in a great roar. It flooded the ground between the tank and mortars with a burning carpet. The carpet swamped the gunners, rising up their bodies, engulfing them in flame, turning them into frenetically writhing human torches, screaming soundlessly, their voices dampened by that awesome fierce crackle.

'Slap it on, Cinders! . . . Give 'em all you've got!' One-Flipper yelled, carried away by the blood-lust and excitement of battle, as the Crocodile rolled over the first mortar position, crushing weapon and men alike, its tracks showering burning fuel to both sides as it rattled on.

Cinders slapped flame to left and right. Even the roar of the gun and the clatter of the Crocodile's tracks could not deaden the inhuman screams of sheer agony now. The mortar-men broke to both sides, rolling themselves in the deep snow in a vain attempt to put out that all-consuming flame. Here and there, those still untouched by the flame started to shoot up their hands. '*Kamerad . . . nicht schiessen . . . habt Erbarmen . . .*'[1]

But this day God was looking the other way. There was to be no mercy. The flame shot out once more and the men, who were as German as they were, were swallowed up by that terrible fire. Five minutes later it was all over. One-Flipper's headset was swamped by the radio calls of success from his armour on both flanks. The men of the von Seydlitz Army had been defeated decisively. The few survivors had thrown away their weapons and fled for the cover of the woods; they would not trouble Battle-Group Flosse any more.

A few minutes after that, the Crocodile, its tracks covered in the bloody gore of the overrun mortar unit, rolled into the courtyard of the big farm to be welcomed by a grinning Schulze and Matz who shouted up to One-Flipper in the turret, 'Well, it worked, sir.'

The SS officer cast a quick glance at the white-clad bodies in the yard, noting that most of them were enemy, and grinned. 'That it did, you rogues,' he called back, as the Crocodile clattered to a halt. 'Captain Mueller'll probably go up the walls when he learns that we deliberately allowed him to be trapped so that we could clear up those bandits once and for all.'

The grins disappeared from the two NCOs' sweat-streaked faces. Swiftly they told One-Flipper what had happened to Mueller. 'Poor unfortunate bastard,' One-Flipper commented, suddenly weary, 'but it was on the cards. He was too inexperienced.'

[1] Comrade . . . don't shoot . . . have mercy.

'Weeds never die,' Matz said, using the old soldier's phrase.

'Yes, weeds never die,' One-Flipper agreed. Stiffly he got out of the turret and dropped to the scuffed, blood-stained snow.

'One thing, sir,' Schulze whispered behind the cover of his big paw, as the three of them started to walk across to the farmhouse to inspect the survivors.

'What's that?'

'We know where the Fat Hermann papers are.'

The look of weariness vanished instantly from One-Flipper's face.

'Where?'

'Big Irmtraut's truck. She's in there now, guarding them with a rolling-pin and a cleaver, as if it was her own virginity.'

One-Flipper's face lit up and he beamed at the two NCOs. 'Now that,' he said, 'is the best news I've heard in many a long day . . .'

FOUR

'But what's so important about those damned papers, sir?' Schulze asked softly, checking that none of the field-mattresses busy now attending to their own wounded were listening. 'For you personally, I mean?'

One-Flipper took a sip of the bitter, ersatz nigger-sweat that one of the gun-girls had offered him, and glanced outside at where his men were preparing the armour for the last stage of their road march to the German lines. 'It's a long story, Schulze,' he said hesitantly.

'We've got time, sir. Matz has got the tankers in hand and Big Irmtraut's pretty well organized in here. But I doubt if we'll be able to move off before dusk. Besides, we don't want to run the risk of a Popov air-strike during daylight.' He paused momentarily. 'Besides, sir, I think that we have . . . a right to know, because we've – that's the fellers from Wotan – have certainly risked having their hooters pushed deep in the crap on this one.'

One-Flipper nodded, his face thoughtful. 'I suppose you have, Schulze. You realize, of course, any knowledge you gain from me could really land you in the shit?'

'I've survived so far . . . I think I'll survive a bit longer.'

One-Flipper made up his mind. He drew a deep breath and said, with an air of finality, 'All right, here we go . . .'

The bombardment had ceased. Slowly, he had raised his head and viewed the steaming new moon-landscape. For a moment he thought he had seen a Russian helmet. But it had only been a small bush, moved by the hot summer wind that blew across the steppe. Cautiously he had got to his feet. The attack had obviously been a failure. The Popovs had been too strong for them once again. But where was the rest of his company?

Staggering forward, his ears still ringing from the bombardment, the long steppe grass wavering in blue ripples in front of his glazed eyes, he had commenced his search. But he hadn't got very far. There had been an explosion. At first he had thought numbly that he had stepped on a mine. Then he had been able to localize the pain; it wasn't in his feet, but in his back, curling hotly around his body as if he had just been beaten by a leather strap. Someone had thrown a grenade at him. He had attempted to reach for his own grenade, but his hand had encountered something wet and hot. He had started to fall. Just before he had blacked out, he had felt his elbow gripped and someone had begun to drag him rapidly across the burningly hot steppe. *But why only one elbow?*

For a while, time was meaningless to him. Life merged into a timeless mixture of pain, the smell of ether and iodine, and long silences, in which he had seemed to hear the soft glide of rubber-soled shoes in the distance. 'We've stopped the damned bleeding,' he had heard once.

Another time he had woken and his nostrils had been assailed by the stink of stale sweat and he had felt a hot burning in his right arm, occasioned, it had seemed, by the tube attached to the bottle suspended above him, through which a bubble had risen at regular intervals.

Once a man in a rubber apron stained with blood had come in and looked down at him for a long time. Before he had disappeared, never to be seen again, he had dropped a handful of jagged crystalline metal cubes on the glass-topped table next to his bed. 'Souvenirs,' he had said, 'took them out of you yesterday.'

Faces had finally started to become familiar. There was the yellow, pudding face of the French orderly, who always stank of garlic, and said 'allo' every time he came through the swing door. There was Kurt, '*Herr Pisspot*', as he called himself, who was responsible for the bedpans. The 'Senior Sister', grim, frightening, and known behind her back as 'Big Knickers'. And there was the '*Frau Doktor*'. Irma Koch was really a 'miss', but all the officer patients called her '*Frau Doktor*'. Tall, blonde, brisk and beautiful, she was compassionate too – a rare quality in wartime military hospitals.

It was she who broke the news to him that the reason the 'allo Frenchman' shaved him in the morning and '*Herr Pisspot*' was always on hand with his bedpan was that he had lost an arm and foot. She wasn't melodramatic about it, nor was she hard-boiled or even flippant, as some military doctors were. She explained the details simply and objectively, those fine level blue eyes of hers fixed on his face the whole while, as if she were afraid that he might break down and sob if she chanced to lose his gaze. 'Your war is over, Major,' she had concluded softly. 'Now you begin a new war, perhaps an even more difficult one – who knows?'

'What do you mean?'

'You will have to live with your disabilities. Create a new life for yourself – and it won't be easy.'

He forced a laugh. 'The SS will take anything these days

that can breathe. They'll find me some rear echelon stallion's job, I'm sure.'

'We will see,' Dr Koch answered. 'Now our first priority is to get well,' and he felt the now familiar tingle of morphia being injected into his one remaining arm.

In spite of the fact that there had seemed no future for him – a regular SS officer with one foot and one arm, who could never command an active battalion again – he had started to get well, for her sake. Somehow or other he had wanted to impress her with his masculinity; the fact that he was not half a man in spite of his terrible wounds.

As a doctor she had approved, he knew that. But he knew too that she did not approve of him as a regular SS officer. He had sensed that when once, high on the cocaine he had now begun to bribe the 'allo Frenchman' to steal for him out of the dispensary in order to deaden his pain, he had grabbed her and tried to kiss her. Dr Koch had pushed him away gently and straightened her rumpled white coat, pulling down her skirt over her excellent, shapely, silk-clad knees. 'It is quite a common phenomenon,' she had said quietly.

'What?'

'A wounded man in convalescence trying to prove his masculinity with a nurse or a doctor.' She had laughed briefly. 'After all, why do you think most of our sisters, who are not exactly beauty queens, are married to young officers?'

Two months after he had been delivered into the hospital, he was allowed up and began to play the nursery games that military hospitals approved as therapy for their patients: draughts, ludo and the like. Now he had begun to dress himself and dispense with the services of the 'allo Frenchman' with the wheel-chair. In the third month, after he had received his crutches, he had invited Dr Koch to accompany him to the cinema and had enjoyed the simple pleasure of actually handling money – for the tram and for the ticket The film had been the usual saccharine-sweet UFA production, with silly songs and girls showing lots of leg, living in that never-never world that the Minister of Propaganda obviously thought was ideal for taking the civilians' minds off the grim realities of total war. He had enjoyed it and he felt that she had too.

But the newsreel – *die deutsche Wochenschau* – had spoiled the whole evening. After the usual war shots there had been one of the customary startling action reports from the front. This time it had been clips of an assault engineer company attacking a Russian bunker on the Eastern Front with flame-throwers. There had been a shot of a Russian soldier running panic-stricken out of the bunker after the first attack. One of the bearded engineers with the round flame-thrower pack on his broad shoulders had gone after the escaping Ivan. The vicious flame had caught up with the fleeing figure. It had run up his earth-coloured uniform until it had streamed from his head and shoulders and then he had collapsed, still burning, and the unseen cameraman had focused on the dying Russian's hideously contorted face. Just for a fleeting fraction of a second. But it had had its effect. In the darkness the audience had gone wild. They had clapped and cheered and someone had bellowed in a thick beery voice, '*Sieg Heil . . . Sieg Heil . . .*'

Then the lights had flicked on and everywhere quite ordinary, dreary civilians had been standing to attention like soldiers, faces gleaming with excitement, their arms outstretched in the 'German greeting'. At his side, Dr Koch had been quietly sobbing. That night he had made love to her for the first time. Tenderly. In the spring of 1944 he had been released from hospital, still hobbling on the cane – that marvellous Malacca cane she had given him – but fit and transferred to a holding battalion, a collection of pasty-faced clerks and 'stomach cases', severely wounded SS men, grouped together in one unit because of the special diet that bad stomach wounds needed. After a week of rusks and milk, forced down with alcohol-free beer, he had had enough. He had asked for a transfer. Regularly each morning he had presented himself to the holding unit commandant, a skinny, yellow-skinned SS colonel, who was kept going by a complicated structure of tubes and splints and who was permanently attached to an evil-smelling bottle at his side, to ask for a posting, and regularly each morning he was turned down; he was needed at the holding unit for 'administrative reasons'. Ten days later he had hobbled out of the barracks, flagged down the first SS vehicle he had seen and ordered the surprised young private to take him immediately to SS Main Headquarters in Berlin. Twenty-four hours later, after a somewhat stormy interview with General Berger, 'the Duke of Swabia', as he was called cynically behind his back, he was on his way to Himmler's Main Battle Headquarters as a temporary staff officer.

They had started to write. Not often, but often enough. On the same day that the Western Allies landed in France, he asked her to marry him. Somewhat to his surprise she accepted him. He had flown back to Berlin and they had been married at the Berlin-Dahlem registry office, one of the dozen or so pairs married that fine June morning, including some very pregnant weeping females whose 'bridegrooms' had died several months earlier. Afterwards he had said, 'You know, Irma, I know nothing really about you, except that you are a doctor – and beautiful.'

Her fine oval face had grown serious for a moment and she had replied, 'Perhaps it would be better if you never came to know anything about me.'

At the time he had paid little attention to the remark; later he was to understand only too well what she had meant.

That evening, just before they set off for a four-day wartime honeymoon in Tangermuende, he met her father for the first time (her mother had been long dead and for some reason unknown to him, Irma spoke little about her). He was a full colonel of the *Wehrmacht*, tall, lean like his daughter, with the purple stripe of the Greater General Staff down the side of his immaculate breeches. He had invited the happy couple to a glass of French champagne in the senior officers' mess at the General Staff HQ in Berlin's *Bendlerstrasse*. But One-Flipper could see he was not particularly happy that his only daughter had married an officer of the Armed

SS. They had toasted each other, the colonel had eyed his battlefield decorations with some approval, offered him the traditional 'thou',[1] and that had been about that. An hour later he had risen to his feet, kissed his daughter and shook One-Flipper's hand. 'I must go now, I'm afraid,' he had announced, 'the war, you know.' With that overwhelming excuse he had disappeared back to his office in the War Ministry, and One-Flipper had never seen him again, save for one last time. And that time had certainly not been a social occasion in any sense of the word.

The news that an attempt had been made on the Führer's life that July burst like a bombshell in Himmler's HQ. Shock had given way to fear, fear to apathy and indecision, and finally, as it had become clear that the Führer had survived the assassination, the urgent desire for revenge and the need to prove one's loyalty to the cause of Adolf Hitler.

Himmler assembled his staff together and roared, his weak, deathly pale face flushed an angry crimson, 'The time has come to deal with those *Wehrmacht* rats in the Bendlerstrasse once and for all. For years now they have been trying to betray us. Now their treachery has to end!' Hurriedly he started rapping out his orders. Every trusted staff officer would be flown into Berlin immediately, report to Goebbels, the club-footed Minister of Propaganda, the senior minister in Berlin, find out about the situation from him and then organize whatever loyal troops there were available to 'liquidate the traitors'. 'And remember, gentlemen,' Himmler had ended his angry tirade, 'shoot first and ask questions later. Those swine in the Bendlerstrasse deserve nothing better!'

Four hours later, after some sporadic shooting in the street outside, One-Flipper at the head of a mixed force of *Luftwaffe* soldiers and the still-loyal Berlin Guards Battalion under the command of a hard-faced Major Remer, a battle-tried veteran, had burst into Army HQ.

[1] Instead of the more formal 'you', the 'thou' form indicates more intimacy between individuals.

Everywhere was in the utmost confusion. Ashen-faced senior officers burnt incriminating papers in their metal waste-paper baskets. Others were already dead, pistols in hand, blood curling down the side of their faces. Some grabbed at their attacking soldiers' arms, screeching their innocence, pleading to be spared before being slammed against the wall by a cruel blow from a brass-bound rifle-butt, while a few frantically attempted to build barricades in the corridors with office furniture and make a fight for it.

But the heart had gone out of most of the men who had conspired against Hitler. At the sight of the excited sweating young soldiers under the command of senior officers, their chests covered with battlefield decorations, they raised their arms wearily and allowed their pistols to be taken from them, knowing that the game was up; their grand plot to kill Hitler and let the Army take over power and thus bring the war to an end had failed. Now the only fate that awaited them was death and their only problem – the manner of their dying.

One-Flipper, still not completely fit, collected his breath after sending a platoon off to guard the Bendlerstrasse's communications centre against any further sabotage and watched while officer after officer came forward to ask for permission to take 'the officer's way out'. Some of them were men who bore the oldest names in the Prussian aristocracy, or whose forefathers had fought in the ranks of the Prussian Army ever since there had been a Prussia. But Major Remer showed no mercy. Time and time again he rapped, 'No', with that tight mouth of his which seemed to be worked by steel springs. 'No, take him away and shoot him in the yard!'

Then One-Flipper's heart had almost stopped beating. Bleeding from a blow to his face, his grey hair hanging down over his forehead, his immaculate uniform ripped open at the collar, a familiar figure approached Remer, who was standing there, booted feet spread wide-apart, hands on his hips, every inch the master of the situation. It was his father-in-law, Colonel Koch!

He addressed Remer with dignity, standing to attention, though he swayed slightly as he did so, 'Respectfully request permission to be given my service pistol and one bullet, *Herr Major*,' he said in a quiet voice, seemingly ignoring the look of contempt on Remer's face and the catcalls of the over-excited young troops, already eager to grab him and place him against the bullet-splattered wall of the yard below.

'Oh yes, *Herr Oberst*, you would respectfully request, wouldn't you? That is the way of you fine gentlemen of the staff with your damned red stripes. First stab our Führer in the back and then expect to get away with a nice, neat, gentleman's death.' He wagged his big finger under Colonel Koch's nose. 'But not with me, my fine sir. You'll be placed against the wall and shot like the treacherous rat you are – '

'Remer,' One-Flipper rapped, not able to stand the humiliation of his father-in-law any longer, 'shut it up!'

Remer swung round and his rat-trap of a mouth dropped open stupidly when he saw who had spoken. 'You?'

'Yes, me. Give him . . .' One-Flipper hesitated a moment, while his father-in-law stared at him, no expression on his ashen face save perhaps curiosity, 'his pistol as he asks.'

'I'll be damned if I will!' Remer exploded. 'Why should he get off any easier than the rest of the red-striped rat-pack?'

'Please!'

'No!'

One-Flipper went for his pistol. 'No,' his father-in-law called. 'No, don't do – '

One-Flipper never heard the rest of his words, nor did he ever see his father-in-law again. But the butt of the Berlin Guardsman's rifle crashed into the back of his head and he went out like a light.

Two days later Himmler personally ordered his court-martial for having 'disgraced the honour of the SS'. The court was lenient on him, at least the President said it was, on account of 'your gallant record in battle and severe physical disability.' He was stripped of all military honours, decorations and awards, including his Knight's Cross, which worried him very little – 'I've cured my throatache years ago,' he confessed cynically to his defending officer[1] – and reduced in rank from major to second-lieutenant; and again he was not overly worried. In a total war, rank was achieved easily.

But it was his personal interview with Himmler, 'under four eyes', as the *Reichsführer* call it, which enlightened him on just how severely he had been punished. After informing him that his father-in-law had been shot by the Berlin Guards Battalion that very same night, Himmler had pursed his lips together in the way he did when he wanted to give the impression that he was weighing his words very carefully and said: 'Since your arrest, Flosse, some very severe abuses, if not direct crimes, have been revealed.'

One-Flipper waited.

'Perhaps they are not sins of commission, but those of omission, as the blacks[2] would say. But sins they are.' He looked severely through his pince-nez at the pale-faced young lieutenant, as if he were a grammar-school teacher censuring a pupil for not having completed his homework. 'Did you know that your dead father-in-law had been married twice?'

'No, *Reichsführer*,' One-Flipper replied, startled by this turn in the conversation into speaking for the first time since he had been ushered into the 'presence'.

'I thought not. You see, it only came out in the subsequent People's Court investigation into the evil-doing of the July criminals. But Colonel Koch had two wives, one dead – and one alive.'

'Alive?'

'Yes, alive and in the United States of America.'

'America?' One-Flipper echoed in amazement.

In spite of his anger, Himmler was pleased by the surprise he had managed to achieve. 'Yes, in America. She fled there in 1933 and after she had divorced Colonel Koch,

[1] The granting of the Knight's Cross which hung round the neck cured the lack of that medal, i.e. throatache.

[2] Blacks=Catholics.

voluntarily I must add, that – er – officer married again. The second wife died in an air-raid on Berlin in 1942.'

'So my wife's mother is still alive, *Reichsführer*?'

'Exactly.' Himmler leaned forward over his big desk, his dark eyes behind the pince-nez boring into One-Flipper's surprised face. 'Yes, how ironic it must be for you to have an American mother-in-law – and a Jewish one to boot.'

'*Jewish?*'

'Yes, Jewish.' Himmler's voice was icy. 'One of my own staff is married to a half-Jew! Now what do you say to that?'

For one long moment One-Flipper could do nothing, save stutter absurdly. 'But . . . but, I didn't know . . . and my wife's papers were in order when they were examined by the SS Genealogical Office. They proved she was of pure Aryan blood from 1760 as the regulations prescribe . . . My wife is a typical –'[1]

Himmler waved him to be silent. 'Lies, all lies. Koch admitted the papers were faked. Such things can be bought on the black market – at a price. Who knows what his reasons were. All that matters now is that one of my key officers, a war hero, is married to a half-Jewess.'

'And my wife?' One-Flipper demanded in sudden alarm.

'Your wife is being taken care of,' Himmler responded primly, as if the matter were of no importance.

'You mean the camps?'

'I mean the camps.'

It was then that One-Flipper dropped his Malacca cane and dived over the big desk to grab a shocked *Reichsführer SS* by the collar, his pince-nez tumbling to one side of his face, fear suddenly in his dark eyes. But in spite of his fear, Himmler still had the presence of mind to press the alarm button at his foot.

The next moment the door was burst open and a wildly struggling One-Flipper was swamped in a half-dozen hefty bodies as the giants of Himmler's bodyguard punched and

[1] SS-men wanting to marry had to prove the 'racial purity' of their future wives before they were allowed to do so.

thumped him in order to make him release his grip on the *Reichsführer*'s throat.

Finally order was restored and a flushed Himmler, tugging at his black tie and returning his pince-nez to its proper position, stared at One-Flipper, restrained by two giants, his face bloody and angry, his breath coming in short hectic gasps as if he had just run a great race. The giants grouped around him, pistols in hand now, and waited for him to pronounce his verdict on ex-Major Flosse. No one had ever laid a finger on the *Reichsführer* and lived since the early days of the Party and the street fights in Munich. There was a few moments of tense, awed expectancy. Even One-Flipper, as confused and bitterly angry as he was, realized that this must be the end of the road for him. But, surprisingly enough, when Himmler finally deigned to speak, his voice was calm and as pedantic as always. 'Lieutenant Flosse,' he intoned. 'In other circumstances I would have absolutely no mercy on you. But I am prepared to take into account certain extenuating circumstances in your case – and you are one of the bravest and most promising of my younger officers. Indeed, some of my corps commanders have always regarded you like Peiper and von Dodenburg as general officer material. Now you will be sent to the SS Punishment Battalion for three months and then we'll see from there . . .' And with that Himmler had dismissed him.

His career, his marriage, perhaps even his life destroyed . . .

One-Flipper sighed wearily and looked out of the window at the soft, sad snowflakes which had begun to drift down again, as if some god on high had decided to bury the miserable, war-torn world down below, banish it from his dismayed gaze for ever. 'Aachen, Arnhem, Huertgen Forest, we went through the lot,' he said after a while. 'Sixty per cent casualties in three months, ten per cent shot at field court-martials for refusal to accept orders or insubordination, twenty per cent desertion. In November last year we finally came out of the line, eighty men left out of eight hundred.

It was then, while the battalion commander searched the jails for fresh cannon-fodder, that Himmler called me to his HQ and offered me this mission.' One-Flipper shrugged. 'What else could I do but accept?'

Matz and Schulze looked at the young officer's weary, sad face. 'If you'll pardon my German, sir,' Schulze commented, 'but it seems to me that the *Reichsheini*'s got you by the short and curlies.'

'And how!' Matz agreed, eyeing the snow morosely.

'I suppose so. At present, she – my wife – is working in the camp hospital at Neuengamme. I think, from the odd letter she manages to get smuggled out, that it's not bad for her there. But God knows what would happen if – ' he broke off suddenly, as if he dare not think that particular thought to an end. 'There are other camps, of course,' he said baldly.

Matz looked at Schulze. The latter nodded. 'Sir, we'll get those damned Goering papers for you, if we have to sacrifice Matz's cherry to Big Irmtraut to do so.'

Matz shuddered violently. 'Don't even think things like that, Schulze! You know how delicate I am.'

'But how are you going to pull that off, you big rogue?' One-Flipper asked, new hope in his eyes. 'She's worse than poor old dead Captain Mueller. She looks after that truck as if it contained all the treasures of the East. Don't you know there's a big padlock on the back of it now, even if you could get Big Irmtraut away from it long enough to get close to the damned thing?'

Schulze winked at him joyfully. 'Sir, the ways of God and Sergeant-Major Schulze are intricate, mysterious and highly successful. I think we are going to have a case of instant love on our hands soon.' He winked wickedly at Matz. 'Don't you think so, my little crippled friend?'

Matz turned pale. 'No, not, *not that*, Schulzi . . .' he quavered,

FIVE

'Have you ever thought what you are going to do after Final Victory, Sergeant Irmtraut?' Matz asked innocently as they lounged in front of the truck containing the papers, regarding the fresh, sparkling snow.

They were alone in the village street, save for a few sentries. The survivors had distributed themselves throughout the village, glad to find warmth and sleep, now that they were safely behind German lines.

'I've never really given it much thought, Corporal,' the massive woman said. 'I volunteered for the Service when I was a mere girl back in '30. Since then I have been concerned with fighting for Final Victory for our Führer Adolf Hitler.' She gave a little sigh at the mention of the leader's name and Matz dodged back out of the way of that alarmingly expanded bosom. 'I have had little time for my personal affairs.'

Matz took a deep breath and whispered a silent prayer for forgiveness to some god, known only to himself. 'But I mean, Sergeant, a fine-looking German woman like yourself must have occasionally thought of meeting the right man, settling down, having a home – and, er . . .' Matz swallowed hard, wondering with that body whether she would need a seven-year gestation period like an elephant, '. . . having children.'

Big Irmtraut blushed to the roots of her moustache. 'I suppose I have,' she answered in a little girl's voice. 'After all, our beloved Führer has often urged us to surrender ourselves – ' her blush deepened to a bright crimson – 'so that the future of the German nation might be assured.'

'Children, kitchen and cooking,' Matz echoed the catchphrase.

She bent her gaze in embarrassment to her enormous feet, enclosed in a pair of stubble-hopper's dice-beakers, the only boots that would fit her. 'Yes.'

Matz caught a glimpse of Schulze sneaking through the snow, a pair of metal-clippers in his big hand. With the clenched fist, he gave the infantry signal for 'attack'. In return Matz poked up his middle finger and silently told Schulze to sit on it. 'I'd like children,' Matz said drily, 'lots of them.' Hesitantly he put his hand on her great paw, where it was dwarfed like that of a baby. 'With the right woman, of course.'

She attempted to withdraw her hand, but he held on to it with all his strength, sweating furiously in spite of the evening cold. 'Of course, I'm not one of your little – er – tarts,' she said, not raising her gaze, but blushing furiously. 'All make-up, cigarettes and silk stockings and the like.'

Matz thought of those enormous red bloomers of hers he had seen on the line at Neustedt and shuddered. 'A German girl neither smokes nor uses make-up, the Führer has said,' he commented hastily.

'Exactly. Our hearts and our bodies must be pure and healthy if we are to bear the soldiers of the future.'

For one frightening moment, Matz had a vision of regiments of fully-grown soldiers, accompanied by tanks and mobile artillery, emerging from Big Irmtraut's womb, instantly ready to do combat. 'One needs a woman one can rely upon,' he said. 'Someone who has been tried, like we have all been tried these last few days in the field of battle, and found not lacking. A woman like you.'

'Corporal Matz,' she breathed, her mighty bosom heaving dangerously. 'Do you really mean that?'

'I have never meant anything more seriously in all my life.' He squeezed her hand and hoped she wouldn't return the pressure; she would crush his fingers to pulp.

'I know nothing about – *love*, Corporal,' she said coyly, fluttering eyelashes that were like miniature Indian punkah-fans. 'But I know it is my duty as a future German mother to learn.' She looked at him directly, her face covered in a deep blush. 'Would you . . . will you teach me, Corporal Matz?'

Suddenly, the little SS man felt very frightened. If she pressed him to her great bosoms, which were now level with his mouth, she'd smother him. 'I'll try, Sergeant Irmtraut.'

'Call me Little Trauti,' she simpered. 'Everyone did when I was a girl.'

'Little Trauti!'

'Egon!' she breathed, and in an excess of romantic emotion attempted to embrace him with those wrestler's arms of hers. Just in time he managed to avoid that killing hug and said urgently, 'But not here, my darling.'

'Of course, of course, I understand, Egon. But where?' Now she was all eagerness, carried away by sex or love, all responsibility for the documents forgotten.

'The barn . . . That one over there.' Matz's words ended in a grunt as she clasped him to her, lifting him completely off his feet. With the frightened little corporal tucked under her mighty arm, his mouth pressing against her enormous right breast like a baby being suckled, she dashed towards the barn, as if she could not wait another instant before she provided her 'beloved Führer' with the children he needed to 'ensure the future of the German nation'.

Schulze grinned as they disappeared at a run into the winter gloom and made the sign of the cross over them. 'God be with you, my children,' he whispered. 'May He make your loins fruitful and your vessels overflow with goodness.' Chortling hugely to himself, the coast at last clear now, he started to work on the truck's padlock . . .

'Christ Almighty!' Matz groaned, holding his swollen burning cheek, as all around him the Wotan survivors made ready to depart. 'She had this sort of string vest on under her knickers, tied up or sewn up between the legs, and I got mixed up in one of the loops. So I got out my knife to cut the shitting loop and she thought I was going to whip off my thing. And she's all over me like a demented dervish, shouting I shouldn't castrate myself for her sake. It was all her fault. She was an evil woman, who had seduced me with her fatal charms.' Matz broke down and shook his head in wonder. 'And then she turned out to be a virgin! What don't I do for Germany!'

Schulze slapped him on the back, so that he would have staggered into the wall if One-Flipper hadn't caught him in time. 'You did a great job of work, you little cripple. I didn't think a little asparagus Tarzan like you would have it in him. Grr, it must have been climbing up the North Face of the Eiger for you to have got over those tits of hers!'

'Well, now we've got the papers,' One-Flipper interrupted happily, checking that everyone was ready to move out. 'Both of you did a good job of work. All right, let's get going. I want to be in Berlin by tomorrow night.'

'Yes,' Matz agreed hastily, 'let's get out of here before she wakes up and finds I'm gone. The way she is I shouldn't be surprised if she didn't rip it off me, roots and all.' He looked fearfully over his shoulder.

Chuckling, Schulze and One-Flipper went out to the waiting vehicles, while above Big Irmtraut snored mightily, a happy smile on her face, now that she had been finally relieved of the burden of her maidenhead, dreaming of hordes of blond-haired children in the brown uniform of the Hitler Youth, each one being patted individually on his golden pate by no less a person than a benign Führer himself. It was one of the best dreams of her whole life.

Four

Fat Hermann takes a Hand

ONE

The great man sat brooding at the far end of the great hall, at the foot of the big marble tomb which contained the mortal remains of his long-dead wife, like a Roman emperor posing in some eighteenth-century classic tragedy. Indeed, in spite of his unclassical figure, he looked a little like a Roman in the green toga-like hunting dress which clothed his enormous girth, with his fat legs encased in bright-green suede boots and his painted fingers, heavy with great gold rings, clutching his hunting dagger in the manner that one of the ancients might have held the short stabbing sword of the legions.

He paid no heed to the heavy tread of the elegant adjutants who halted at the far end of the hall. Nor did he seem to notice the distraught woman with the ladders in her field-grey woollen stockings and with circles under her eyes from weeping, who seemed strangely out of place among the immaculately dressed aides. One of them coughed.

Nothing happened. The great man continued to stare at the tomb of his dead Swedish wife, around which he had built this great edifice before the war and which he must now destroy in order that the Reds would not enjoy the triumph of having it fall into their dirty hands. Karin's Hall would never be communist!

'*Herr Reichsmarschall!*' the tallest adjutant risked the words.

Slowly, very slowly, again like a character in a classical drama, Reich Marshal Hermann Goering, Head of the German *Luftwaffe*, turned his great head, as if it was taking his drug-crazed brain a long time to become aware of the direction from which the words had come. He stared at the officer who had spoken with dull, glazed eyes, sucking the great ruby which decorated his pudgy thumb with his red-painted lips. Finally he said, 'Yes?'

'This woman soldier from the 104th *Luftwaffe* Field Signals Company wishes to speak with you, sir,' the adjutant said, trying to forget that the bloated pervert opposite him had once been a keen young fighter ace, the winner of Imperial Germany's highest award and the last commander of the immortal Richthofen Squadron, itself.

Goering did not look at the distraught Big Irmtraut. Speaking to the adjutant, he said hollowly, his voice weak and distraught, 'Is it important, Captain?'

'I think it is, sir. Otherwise I wouldn't have disturbed your – er – devotions.'

'What does it concern?'

'Your personal war diary, sir, and various other important personal papers.'

A vague interest seemed to stir in his violet eyes. He took his lips from the ruby fingers he had been sucking and waved the pudgy hand languidly at Big Irmtraut. 'She has my permission to approach.'

Flanked by the adjutants, Big Irmtraut strode forward, her heavy boots echoing hollowly on the black-and-white tiles of the mausoleum. She came to attention, stamping down her right foot and in doing so succeeded in breaking one of her suspenders so that her torn woollen stocking tumbled down over her boot. Goering stared at it for what seemed a long time, as if he could not quite understand what had happened. 'She may speak,' he commanded in the end.

The big captain nodded at Big Irmtraut, whose misery had vanished in face of the exotic sight before her. In her best military manner the huge woman recounted her story; how while she and a 'treacherous friend' had been discussing 'a personal problem', other 'traitors' had abused her 'good nature and trust' to break into the truck containing the Reich Marshal's papers and war diary.

When she was finished there was a heavy silence, while the officers waited for one of Fat Hermann's celebrated outbursts. But none came. Instead, Goering took a handful of diamonds out of his pouch, which he affected in the style of a medieval hunter, and played with them a while like a boy with his marbles, his whole attention seemingly devoted to counting the gems and sorting them into their various colours.

It was only when the tall captain had cleared his throat several times that he said, 'Ask her who those traitors were who stole the papers.'

'The SS, *Herr Reichsmarschall*,' Big Irmtraut answered promptly. 'A group of lecherous SS men, who have nothing in their heads but treachery and the seduction of poor innocent girls.' Suddenly the thought that she had surrendered her precious virginity, which she had guarded so zealously for forty years, overcame her and she began to sob.

'*SS . . . SS . . . SS . . . SSSSSS*,' Goering repeated the initials over and over again, until the adjutants began to shuffle their feet nervously and look at each other uneasily, wondering whether Fat Hermann was going to have another of his 'nervous attacks', as his raving fits of madness were called delicately by his staff.

Suddenly the fat Marshal sat bolt upright, his face stern, eyes clear and hard. 'A uniform,' he snapped, clicking his fat fingers impatiently. 'A uniform for fighting. I feel in a combative mood. Quick . . . *quick!*' His voice rose shrilly like a hysterical woman. 'There is no time to be lost.' Before Big Irmtraut's amazed gaze, a huge bearskin robe appeared as if from nowhere, under which the adjutants disrobed their master until he stood there in his silk underwear, legs mottled black and blue, the result of years of drug injections. Now another adjutant hurried in, several uniforms draped over his outstretched arms for Goering's inspection. Goering rejected them one by one as the adjutant proffered them. 'The black. God in heaven, no! Not *their* colour. *The white?* Purity is out of the question at the moment. We have dirty work on our hands, gentlemen. Green? No, it will not go with my colour in my present mood of indignation. Ah, yes, the purple . . . Yes, that is the correct colour. *The royal purple!* That's it. For am I not the heir apparent? Quick, gentlemen, dress me.' He stamped his right foot like a petulant child and the fat rippled the length of his gross body, ending at the jowls which continued to tremble long after the adjutants began to fit him into the uniform of his own design.

Finally he was dressed in the gleaming rich purple uniform, both breasts of the tunic covered with so many gold and silver decorations that Big Irmtraut had to narrow her eyes to slits against the glare.

Poised there imperiously, pudgy hand gripping his marshal's staff, heavy with gold and jewels, as if he were posing for some nineteenth-century heroic portrait painter, Goering made his plans.

'That chicken farmer Himmler is behind it all. I know it – *here*!' He smote his chest. 'When the time comes, he wants to succeed to the throne. But that little jumped-up clerk will have to get up earlier in the morning if he is to catch Hermann Goering out, oh yes indeed!' He beamed confidently around his silent bemused audience. 'Now this is what is to be done. Reconnaissance, Deschner! I want to find out which route the SS are using to get to Berlin.'

'Sir!' The officer in question stamped to attention, gave a half bow, and left, presumably to alert a reconnaissance squadron.

'Dive-bombers. Herber, where is Rudel, Colonel Rudel?' He snapped his fingers impatiently.

'Colonel Rudel is presently testing the new Me 262 at Gatow Field, sir,' Captain Herber replied, wondering why Goering was interested in the whereabouts of the one-legged, dive-bombing ace.

'Excellent. Couldn't be better. Get him. Once reconnaissance have identified the position of these SS bandits, Rudel will take them out.'

'Take them out, sir!' Herber gasped. 'But the roads all over Brandenberg are packed with refugees, sir, now the

Russians have started their new offensive. If Colonel Rudel attempts to bomb these SS people, our civilians must invariably . . .' His voice died away. Goering was no longer listening.

Striding towards an open-mouthed Big Irmtraut, one of his many medals held outstretched by its ribbon, he said, 'My daughter, you have saved the empire.' Pressing the surprised field-mattress down on one dirty knee, he draped the medal solemnly around her neck. 'We thank you!' And with that he stalked back to the chair and recommenced his brooding over the tomb of a woman who had been dead for nearly a decade . . .

TWO

It seemed as if the whole of Eastern Germany was on the move. Everywhere the refugee columns, the *treks*, as they were called, blocked the roads, crawling painfully slowly towards the West, fleeing before the advancing Russians who were slaughtering, raping, burning and pillaging their way into the Reich. Hungry, frozen and weary, they plodded on foot along the ice-glazed roads under sub-zero temperatures, or if they were lucky trundled westwards in farm-carts, covered with tarpaulins, through which the chimneys of stoves had been poked. It was an evacuation of incredible suffering, akin to the folk migrations of the fourth century, which brought millions of Germans from their homes in the East for good, but there was no thought of ceasing that terrible flight. The spectre of the Red Army and the horrific retribution they would wreak on any German they captured drove them ever onwards.

Huddled in the turret of the Crocodile together with One-Flipper, Schulze and Matz crawled along with the rest, minds numbed by the freezing cold, their only concern the civilians attempting to infiltrate their column on foot or with one of their slow, horse-drawn carts. Berlin was only some forty kilometres away, yet at the snail's pace they were being forced to move it might just as well have been forty light years away. Hour after hour they groaned on in low gear, urinating over the side of the vehicle or heating a can of food on the engine cowling, for they dare not stop and lose their position in that great slow snake crawling miserably towards the capital.

Tragedy struck time and time again. A horse collapsed and the old woman guiding it could not get it back on its feeble legs again. The column swept by her on both sides, as she sat there weeping and stroking the dying animal's face with her skinny withered hand. A baby was born dead and was flung out of one of the moving trek carts wrapped in newspaper by one of the women attending the moaning mother. An old man went mad, ran screaming joyously across the snowy field bordering the road and then walked back quietly and squatted at the roadside, face in hands, watching the carts trundle by like some peasant watching big-city traffic returning from some peacetime Sunday outing.

Schulze shook his head and tugged at the end of his frost-bitten nose, trying to get some life back into it. 'We're finished,' he remarked grimly, almost as if he were speaking to himself. 'There's no hope for Germany now.' Matz nodded.

One-Flipper clicked open his cane, took out his last cigar, broke it solemnly into three pieces, and handed them a piece each. 'Now it's every man for himself,' he said quietly, as the three of them lit up. 'It's a question of survival.' He tried to force a smile, warming a little to the thought that soon he might well be able to achieve Irma's release from Neuengamme. 'We've survived so far, the three of us, and after the kind of shit we've come through these last few years, I don't doubt we'll be able to do so again. '

'You never know with the SS, sir,' Matz said gloomily, the choice cigar not able to rid him completely of his mood of despair. 'The Black Guards never know when to give up.'

'Sign a separate peace,' One-Flipper began and then stopped suddenly. There was a low drone coming from the west, getting closer by the instant.

Everywhere white anxious faces, civilian and military, turned skywards in an attempt to locate the plane. 'There . . . over there at two o'clock!' Schulze cried, pointing with his gloved hand at the dark shape coming in to their left, squat, intent and sinister against the leaden-grey snow sky.

One-Flipper said a silent prayer and then the plane was upon them, zooming in at two hundred and fifty kilometres an hour, filling the sky with its howl, roaring over the long weary column at tree-top height.

Schulze caught a quick glimpse of the twin engines and the black and white crosses under its wings and cried as it hurtled up into the sky once more. 'Don't piss yersens! It's one of ours! Junkers 88 – recce plane!'

Matz breathed out a heart-felt sigh of relief. 'Oh, my aching back, I can feel the urine trickling down my left boot! I thought it was a Popov.'

'Good God, don't even mention the word, Corporal,' One-Flipper said emphatically. 'The very thought gives me the dry heaves. What a mess they'd make of this column.' Curiously he watched as the Junkers came in again, roared the length of the column once more and then just before it broke off its run and climbed skywards again, dropped two flares which burst and started to burn a bright red on the snowy field to their right, colouring it a blood-red ominous hue.

'Now what do you make of that, sir?' Matz asked, as the Crocodile came level with the first of the spluttering flares, while the plane now began to disappear into the distance.

'Search me, Corporal. It's a recognition signal of course, but for whom? Not for us. Why would we need it?'

Fifteen minutes later, as the short winter afternoon started to give way to night, another Junkers reconnaissance plane came in and repeated the strange performance, again leaving red flares burning in the fields on both sides of the column.

Matz shuddered and said quickly, 'A louse just ran over my liver,' while One-Flipper stared up at the darkening sky and the rapidly disappearing plane with a worried frown on his face, as the column crawled on, each person in it now oppressed by a strange and frightening sense of apprehension.

As the drivers began to flick on their convoy lights prior to night driving, another Junkers dived from the sky and repeated the strange performance. Now Schulze could not hide his fears any longer. 'You don't think that even *they* would do that, sir, do you? Not with these civvies everywhere. Surely not!'

'What exactly do you mean, Sergeant-Major?' One-Flipper forced himself to ask, though he knew, with a sinking feeling, exactly what Schulze meant.

'Look, sir,' Schulze answered urgently, 'let's not kid each other. I think we're gonna have our dicks in the wringer right soon. We've flogged *Luftwaffe* documents of vital importance, somehow Fat Hermann's got to know – perhaps from Matzi's only true love here – '

Matz pulled a sour face.

'And now Fat Hermann's gonna to do something about it. Why else those crates and the flares? They're not exactly there to light our way home, you know, sir.'

'Yes, yes . . .' One-Flipper cried in frustration, already dimly aware of the strange howl in the far distance, 'but what are we going to do if – ' he stopped short.

'Absolutely no cover, sir,' Schulze said, waving his hand at the flat darkening landscape, bare of trees or any other hiding place. 'If they come – '

'*When*,' Matz interrupted firmly, his gaze sweeping the horizon to their front, trying to ascertain from whence that strange howl came.

'*When* then, we abandon the vehicles,' Schulze concluded.

'But the Goering papers, Schulze,' One-Flipper protested in an agony of despair, knowing that he was going to have to make a decision about Irma's fate. 'Without those papers, all this has been for nothing.'

'I know that, sir,' Schulze snapped harshly. 'But I've the lives of my men to consider. And what can we do here? We're sitting ducks out here.'

One-Flipper hung his head in defeat. 'All right, Sergeant-Major,' he said hoarsely. 'When they come, you can order the men to abandon the vehicles. After all that's all they're after.' He turned away to hide the tears in his eyes.

Colonel Rudel clenched his heavy fighter's jaw and felt himself at one with the Messerschmitt, physically sensing the great power under his control as the experimental jet hissed over the land, drawing a huge evil shadow behind it across the empty snowfields. All the while his keen eyes searched the horizon, looking for the convoy with the armoured vehicles somewhere in its centre that the recce planes had pinpointed.

Rudel, the one-legged dive-bombing ace, had no compunction about bombing a convoy which was made up of his fellow countrymen. He had been personally told by Goering over the radio phone that they were traitors and deserved death. But even without that knowledge, Rudel would kill. It was his profession and he enjoyed it; after six years of war he had no scruples of that nature left.

'Colonel . . . Colonel . . .' the voice of his wingman crackled across his space.

He pressed his throat-mike. 'Heinz?'

'To port, Colonel,' young Heinz's excited voice reported. 'Down there to port, sir!'

Rudel's keen hunter's gaze swung round. Yes, there they were all right: a long miserable dark worm of humanity moving incredibly slowly across the snowy waste. And half-way down the column, hemmed in by peasant carts drawn by horses and oxen, was the armour he had been ordered to knock out. He grinned wolfishly. It would be as easy as stealing a lollipop off a blind kid. 'Heinz, we'll buzz them first and then on the second run come in for the attack. Remember, boy, from rear to front and don't miss. Third and last run the incendiaries. Clear?'

'Clear, Colonel.'

'All right then. *Now!*'

The two-engined plane came roaring in at 600 kilometres an hour, the howl of its motors ripping the evening silence apart fearsomely, drowning the screams, the cries of fear, the curses of the suddenly alarmed peasants. Schulze flung a glance upwards just in time to catch a fleeting glimpse of the iron crosses under the wings of the planes, the like of which he had never seen before. But he recognized danger when he saw it. 'Bale out!' he yelled urgently into his radio mike. '*BALE OUT EVERYWHERE!*'

Just as the second plane came barrelling in, swirling up a wake of flying snow from the fields on both sides of the suddenly stalled convoy, Schulze flung himself over the side of the Crocodile. Everywhere, the men of Wotan were doing the same, flinging themselves from their vehicles and pelting heavily across the snow as far away from the road as they could get, watched by the amazed bewildered peasants who could not understand why German soldiers should run away from German planes. They would soon find out.

In a great wide curve, Rudel brought his plane round and into position once more, trailing huge brown bursts of smoke behind him. He touched the throat-mike. 'Going in for the run now, Heinz,' he snapped. 'Keep on my tail and aim low. Over and out!'

His eyes narrowed to slits and his jaw clenched pugnaciously, Rudel concentrated on the attack, feeling that old familiar thrill, that almost sexual urge in his loins. He throttled back, feeling the great plane shudder under his grip. 'Hold it, hold it . . .' he whispered, as if he were talking to a live thing, his big capable hands holding the plane easily. Now the convoy was looming up ever larger. He could see the first of the armoured vehicles quite clearly now, in spite of the gloom, and all around it the white blurr of faces looking up at him curiously. The sight irritated him. 'Get the hell out of the way,' he roared, 'you're putting me off my aim.' Then he forgot the civilians and concentrated on his target, as the *Char B* filled the whole gleaming circle of the firing sight, criss-crossed by the fine calibrated lines. '*NOW!*' and pressed the firing button.

The whole plane trembled violently and for one fleeting second the recoil of that tremendous volley seemed to stop the Messerschmitt in mid-air and then it was rushing on to the next target, leaving behind it a shattered smoking French tank and a suddenly panicked group of civilians scrambling feverishly for cover.

'There she goes, Cinders!' Schulze yelled above the chatter of the cannon and the snarling whine of the jet motors, as a cannonshell struck the fuel trailer of the Crocodile. 'NOW YOU'LL HAVE TO PLAY WITH YOURSELF. YOUR TOY'S GONE!' He bellowed as the flame-thrower fuel exploded with a huge whoosh.

'My God,' One-Flipper, crouched in the snow next to the panting NCOs, groaned. 'They've got the documents!'

They had indeed. A burst of cannon-fire had ripped down the length of the half-track carrying them, stitching gleaming metallic holes its whole length and ripping the engine into steel shreds.

'Perhaps the documents won't be too dam – ' Matz began and then ducked hastily as the two jets came in for their third run, this time without firing cannon. But this time something more deadly came from the Messerschmitts. A myriad round eggs tumbled from their stomachs to burst with a spurt of flame below.

'Incendiaries!' Schulze yelled as the first plane completed its run, leaving vehicle after vehicle behind it burning instantly in a fierce, white spluttering light. 'Phosphorus! Thank God we're over here. That stuff sticks to anything.' Next to him Matz shuddered. He had once seen the result of a Tommy phosphorus attack on his native Berlin. The chemical had clung to the flesh of the poor souls who had been struck by it to the end. The only way to get it off had been surgically. As soon as the person afflicted was removed from water, his flesh had begun to burn again. Matz swallowed fearfully and felt tempted to hide his head in the snow. Instead he forced himself to watch as the second pilot came in to complete the havoc and destruction wrought by the leader.

But Lt. Heinz was rattled. It was his first low-level straffing attack and Rudel was a hard task-master. Too late, he heard Rudel's gasp over the intercom, and then the harsh command, '*Stop bombing! . . . Heinz, for God's SAKE . . .*'

The first cluster landed right in the middle of a bunch of men and women crouching behind a low stone wall some fifty metres away from the stalled burning convoy. There were faint puffs of smoke everywhere. Tiny white particles of phosphorus splattered upwards in deadly showers, striking the huddled civilians all over. Immediately they started to burn, their clothes, their skins, their hair.

The terrified, panic-racked victims leapt around in a frenzy, tearing at their burning clothes with hands that were burning themselves. Their hair ablaze and writhing in agony as the flames burned into their skulls, they ripped out the hair in great handfuls, shrieking like banshees and throwing themselves into the snow only to find it did not extinguish the flames. They ran until they could run no more and crumpled to the ground to burn away into charred lumps.

It was too much for Matz. Ignoring the incendiaries flying everywhere, he raised his machine pistol and took quick aim. 'You rotten fly-boy bastard!' he screamed, the foam flying from his lips, his eyes crazy. '*Take that!*'

The savage burst of fire ripped the whole length of the Me 292's ugly grey belly, ran into its cockpit. It staggered visibly in mid-air, bits of metal flying from it in a steel rain. Abruptly a sheet of sickening yellow flame shot from its port engine. Immediately it went dead. A wing broke off. It tumbled to the ground like a great gleaming leaf.

Schulze caught a glimpse of the pilot's ashen face as he frantically struggled to keep the stricken plane airborne. But there was no hope of that now. At six hundred kilometres an hour it streaked to the ground. With a huge, echoing crash it struck the field to their right and disintegrated in a great ascending ball of fire. Up above, Rudel shrugged and then reached for his radio to report the success of his mission to Goering; he'd need a new wingman. Below, an unutterably weary and broken One-Flipper started to progress from one victim of the incendiary attack to the other, waiting for them to remain still for a brief moment so that he could put an end to their terrible misery with his pistol. His pistol cracked time and time again.

They were no longer human beings. They were animals of a kind he had never encountered before. Their gleaming white teeth, brilliant against the charred skin of their faces, snapped together with grisly skeletal clicking sounds. Caught up in the ultimate horror of man's inhumanity to man, they shrieked and screamed, cursing the God who had created them, praying for death to relieve them from their terrible suffering. Time and time again.

And the roof of the truck containing the Hermann Goering papers, that had meant so much to him, burnt steadily in solemn finality . . .

THREE

They arrived in Berlin the following night. There was very little traffic in the streets: the occasional wood-burning truck and a couple of late cyclists, probably returning from the evening shift.

The city was completely blacked-out and the clatter of the horses' hooves, which pulled the two carts laden with the weary Wotan men, echoed and re-echoed among the stark sombre outlines of the bomb-ruins everywhere. Yet there was life in the ruins. Occasionally a door opened and a knife of yellow light slid into the blackness, accompanied by a burst of hearty male laughter or the drunken giggle of a woman.

'Red-light district,' Schulze announced in the leading cart apropos of nothing. 'Knocking shops as far as the eye can see.'

'What good's slit to us?' one of the soldiers sprawled out in the dirty lice-ridden straw complained. 'I ain't eaten for thirty-six hours. I couldn't get it up – even if Greta Garbo and her sister played with my dong.'

'Don't worry, soldier-boy,' Schulze replied easily, whipping up the reins and urging the weary nag to one last effort, 'you'll get your fodder and a bit of the other as well before this night is out . . . Gee up, you four-legged arse with ears. Gee up!'

Ten minutes later the two carts arrived at their destination, a large noisy house in the midst of a stone waste of bombed ruins. 'Are we here?' One-Flipper queried without interest.

'We are. And as a good NCO it is now my duty to see my men bedded down for the night before I attend to my own modest wishes.' Schulze guffawed hugely at some private joke and then snapped, in high good humour, 'Ape-turd, cover me!'

Together they dropped to the pavement, Matz with his machine pistol unslung, and went stiff-legged towards the big house. Confidently, as if he had been there before, Schulze rapped on the door three times and waited. Not for long. Light appeared, there was a whispered conversation at the door, Schulze and Matz disappeared. Ten minutes later a grinning Matz, an open bottle of champagne in his hand now instead of his machine pistol, appeared chortling gleefully. 'All right, you bunch of wet-tails, get the lead out of yer butts. There's steak for everybody, as much booze as yer want, and for any of you who isn't a warm brother, *there's slit*!'

The men's exhaustion vanished in an instant. Whooping

and cheering, they dropped from the carts and rushed to the open door, while Matz, already a little drunk from the champagne, held up his hand gallantly to help One-Flipper to descend.

'But how did that big rogue do it?' One-Flipper asked surprised, as he entered the brothel and viewed the entrance hall lit by heavy Moorish lamps and draped with purple tapestries.

'Sergeant-Major Schulze managed to organize something when he broke into Goering's papers that night, sir,' Matz said a little hesitantly, as they went down the hall to the sound of excited male laughter and the lighter tones of women, many women.

'What for instance?' One-Flipper's amazement even overcame his mood of despair.

'This.' Matz opened his hand to reveal a single gem gleaming in the middle of his dirty palm.

'Good God, a diamond!'

'Yes, he found five of them tucked away in the filing cabinet. Fat Hermann must have played with them like a horny schoolboy plays with his eggs. This lot's costing us one of them. Come on, sir!'

As they entered the main room, filled with excited soldiers and half-dressed whores and heavy with the smell of cheap perfume and Turkish cigarettes, a large woman with frizzed hair and heavy painted eyelids, whose massive breasts threatened to burst out of the tight black silk confines of her low-cut dress, came to meet them, beringed pudgy hands outstretched. '*Amis*,' she simpered from her rosebud mouth, '*les braves soldats allemands!*'

'Come off the Frog, Bertha,' Matz said scornfully. 'The only bit of Frog about you is the Parisians you put over yer customers' dongs.'

'Naughty boy,' the Madame said and gave Matz a playful tap across the cheek which nearly knocked his mouth from the neck of the champagne bottle he was attempting to drink from, 'mustn't give away poor Bertha's trade secrets, must we? Everyone knows you horny German soldiers like *l'amour Française.'* She smiled winningly at One-Flipper and indicated the two girls standing behind her, one large, heavy, blonde and very German, the other dark and brooding with a lot of make-up. '*For M'sieu l'officier* one of the two best I have, or if the gentleman wishes – ' she gave a great gallic shrug – 'both my *petite choux.*'

One-Flipper shrugged and slumped down wearily at the nearest table. 'No, thank you, Bertha, something to drink will do – and when my men have been fed – ' he indicated the starving Wotan men, who were wolfing down the steaks, holding them in one hand, with their other arm around the whores – 'perhaps something to eat.'

'At your command, my gallant soldier,' Bertha cried, '*à bientôt.*' She turned and waddled to the bar to pass on One-Flipper's order, while Matz whooped and grabbed both girls, crying, 'Now then, my passion pussies, what about enjoying yourselves tonight like you've never enjoyed yersens before? Let Corporal Matz show you the way to paradise, my darling.' And with that, the three of them, giggling uproariously, disappeared up the nearby stairs.

Schulze returned from his own journey upstairs to find One-Flipper sitting alone and morose in the midst of that noisy scene, staring at his glass of champagne, shoulders hunched as if he bore all the cares of the world. His happy look vanished and he finished buttoning up his flies hurriedly. 'No good, sir?' he asked, sitting down next to the officer.

'Of course, Schulze, as usual you have done an excellent job. The men needed this, though I doubt if the ordinary quartermaster-bull would approve of your form of billet – and the expense.' One-Flipper forced a weary smile.

'No, I doubt it too, sir. But in a way I want nothing to do with the military authorities for the time being. That's why we're staying here as long as we remain in Berlin. I've already fixed it with Big Bertha.'

One-Flipper looked at him curiously. 'What exactly do

you mean? We'll have to report in to the military authorities somewhere along the line. We need pay, rations, you know the sort of thing. Hell, they might well class us as deserters if we don't contact HQ eventually.'

Schulze waved away one of the whores who was attempting to approach their table, swaying dangerously as she did so. 'Later, my beloved,' he said routinely. 'Later, try to contain yourself till then.' He turned back to One-Flipper. 'But why do we have to, sir? We can obtain all the rations we need through Big Bertha here. She's preparing her own little escape fund and diamonds fit very well into it.'

'There is still the question of being posted as deserters, Schulze,' One-Flipper objected.

'Yes, *if* HQ knows we are alive. But do they?' He let that thought sink in, and then continued. 'Look at it like this. After those planes took us out, you can imagine what Fat Hermann did. He flew to Berlin to have it out with the *Reichsheini*. Himmler, as I see it, would now like to see the whole nasty mess dead and buried – after all he did try to stab one of his closest colleagues in the back.' He hesitated a moment. 'And if my reasoning is correct, he'd like to see us, or more particularly, *you*, buried with it.'

'But why?'

'Because you know too much, sir, and he knows that because of that business with your wife he can no longer rely upon you to keep your mouth shut. Therefore it would be better . . .' He didn't finish the sentence; he clicked his forefinger back and forth, as if he were pulling the trigger of a rifle.

One-Flipper nodded grimly. 'Of course, you're right. That four-eyed bastard Himmler knows only loyalty to himself.'

'Not only him, sir,' Schulze said, taking his eyes off a naked whore doing something impossible with a champagne bottle to the accompaniment of delighted cheers from the men of Wotan watching her obscene act, 'the lot of them. All the golden peasants and the brown bigshots – they're out for number one. They know the war's lost and they're making provisions one way or the other so that they can emerge from it with their Persil tickets.'[1]

'You sound like a Bolshy.'

'Perhaps, sir. But what front-swine wouldn't be a Bolshy in January 1945, when he knows that soon he's gonna be dropped in the shit from a great height while big animals get away with it, ready to kiss Churchill's arse and pull Stalin's plonker for him if necessary?'

One-Flipper nodded. 'I suppose you're right, Schulze. But what can hairy-arsed stubble-hoppers like us do about it? We've had our eggs in a rat-trap right from the start, way back to 1939.'

Schulze shook his head firmly, his big honest face hard and set. 'I fought the bastards right from the start. Nobody, *but nobody*, is taking Mrs Schulze's only son for a ride.'

'My wife . . .' One-Flipper began miserably, but Schulze held up his hand for silence.

'Sir, with all due respect, you've still got eggshell behind yer spoons in these matters, 'cos you're an officer and a gent. You want yer missus out of Neuengamme. All right, why not do it direct, instead of having to kiss that chicken-farmer's kester to get her out?'

'What do you mean?' One-Flipper sat up, the defeat vanishing from his eyes to be replaced by a look of guarded new hope.

'Sir, we have got these,' he opened his hand to reveal the three gems resting in his big palm, 'this,' he clenched his fist, 'and this!' He tapped his forehead. 'Together me, you and my boys of the Wotan could carry your missus out of Neuengamme.'

One-Flipper looked at him incredulously. 'You don't mean . . .'

'I do.'

'But how?'

'I don't know how myself, sir . . . *yet.* But there is a place in Hamburg where anybody who knows his way about the

[1] A German expression indicating that the owner is as white as if he had been washed with Persil washing powder.

waterfront can get anything he wants.'

'And what place is that?' One-Flipper asked, hardly able to believe that there was still hope for him and Irma.

'The Dead Zone, sir . . .'

FOUR

In small, cautious groups, cleanly shaven now and their uniforms pressed by the Berlin whores, the men of Wotan left the battered railway station at Hamburg's Rothenburgsort station and started to follow Schulze, Matz and One-Flipper towards what the big Hamburger NCO called the 'Dead Zone', keeping a look-out for inquisitive patrols of chaindogs and the local *schupos.* It was getting dark now and as the crowds of yellow-faced, starving, shabby workers hurrying home to the suburbs thinned, the patrols thickened accordingly. At night, the centre of bomb-shattered Hamburg was a dangerous place to be, occupied by whores, pimps, black-marketeers, deserters – and murderers.

As they walked through the stone waste of what had once been a thriving industrial area, Schulze told the other two how the place had got its strange name; how after the great week-long Allied raids of July 1943, the whole area of Rothenburgsort, and the adjoining districts of Hammerbrook and South Hamm, where the civilians had been killed in their thousands in Operation Gomorrah, as the Tommies had called the raids, had been sealed off by the Hamburg authorities. Unable to deal with hundreds of unburied dead still trapped in the deep cellars of the area, they had sealed off whole streets with the debris and barbed wire. They had been afraid that the hitherto undreamed-of accumulation of corpses would give rise to a plague comparable to that of 1895 when a third of the city had gone down with cholera.

'That July the decontamination squads, clearing up the stiffs, had to go in wearing gas masks, where the filter had been removed and replaced by a pad soaked in rum or cognac,' Schulze said. 'Otherwise they wouldn't have been able to have stood the stink. Most of them were pissed for days on end. But even then they couldn't cope with all the stiffs, and besides, the golden peasants didn't want the rest of the city to see just how many stiffs there were. So that's how the Dead Zone came about. Only, of course, there's others beside the dead here.'

'Knock it off, Schulze!' Matz snapped, as their boots echoed hollowly in the darkening ruins, flashing a look behind him, as if he half-expected a walking stiff to be creeping after him. 'You'll have me pissing in me boot in a minute.' He shuddered. 'You mean under that stuff there, there are dead bodies everywhere?'

Schulze nodded grimly. 'Exactly, my little shit-scared friend. And underneath us, too. The cellars are full of stiffs, so they say.'

'Christ on a crutch, then we're walking over dead bodies!' Matz breathed. 'Come on, Schulze, change the subject won't you. Tell us something cheerful.'

'There's nothing cheerful about the Dead Zone.' He sniffed, and addressed himself to One-Flipper as the shadows lengthened even more and they progressed deeper into the abandoned area. 'Now, sir, who would you try to tap if you wanted to know something about a C-Camp?'

The officer looked puzzled. 'The guards, perhaps. They belong to the General SS, so we'd have an opening there.'

Schulze looked scornful. 'I hardly think, sir, they'd be likely to tell us how to crack their own camp.'

'No, of course, you're right, Schulze. But the prisoners – well, I mean, they're not *available*.' One-Flipper's face fell a little as he thought of his wife Irma, now only a matter of kilometres away, yet as remote as if she were on the moon.

'Yes, but those prisoners do have contacts on the outside. And if they have those contacts, this is the place where I think we'll find them, sir.'

'What do you mean by contacts, Schulze?' Matz asked,

keeping very close to the other two and frequently throwing nervous glances over his shoulder.

'Well, you know camps, Matzi. There's always an inmate wanting to smuggle himself out and there's always a screw or some working stiff – an electrician, plumber, somebody like that – who is prepared to do it for them – for a consideration.'

'All right, I'll buy that, Schulze. But why do you think we'll find those contacts here?'

'Yes, why?' One-Flipper asked too.

'Because those C-Camps contain commies, socis, yids, warm brothers and that kind of poor sod – and in the Dead Zone, you'll find all those types. They'll know how to get things out from their own kind behind Swedish curtains – and *in*.'

Almost as if on cue, a high-pitched affected voice cooed from the darkness of the ruined building to their left, 'Hello, soldier boys, looking for a nice time?'

Matz jumped and swung round hastily. 'Oh, thou holy strawsack!' he gasped at the sight that met his eyes there.

Poised in the doorway there was a gross caricature of a woman: a burly figure clad in a low-necked rayon jersey, artificial breasts moulded by a ferocious bra into bullet-like projectiles, tight black skirt, slit on one side to reveal black net stockings and a suspicion of a garter, which clashed strangely with the large boots.

'The fairy queen himself!' Schulze said, finally managing to recover his lost speech.

'That's right, handsome,' the caricature said without offence. 'Is that a pistol in your pocket or are you just glad to see me?' It giggled uproariously at its own humour and fobbed Schulze with a limp-wristed blow. 'Call me Marlene, darling. I'm doing my Dietrich this week.' Marlene looked at their silver SS insignia in the fading light without any apparent fear and then asked, 'And what are you SS boys out for this night – protection, perversion or a piss-up? We can give the lot in the Dead Zone, you know.'

'Neither,' Schulze said, knowing that Marlene, true to his

type, would be the ideal person to supply him with the leads he needed before it got completely dark. 'Information.'

'Info.' Marlene's seductive look vanished, as did the careful way in which he pouted his blood-red lips. 'That could be dangerous. But what kind of information do you need?'

Schulze took the plunge. Swiftly casting a look behind him and noting that his men, vets that they were, had carefully and quietly taken up their positions in the ruins on either side of the street, he said, 'Information about Neuengamme.'

'Neuengamme. You mean the CC there?' Marlene asked.

'Exactly.'

The affected tone had gone from Marlene's voice to be replaced by a deep masculine bass when he spoken again. 'That's a pretty hot iron, brother.'

'Perhaps, *brother*. But it's worth some Marie to us to find out.'

'How many pieces of cabbage are you prepared to pay?'

Schulze dug into his back pocket and brought out a thick wad of twenty-mark notes, which Big Bertha had given him for another of the diamonds for her escape fund. Carelessly he peeled off five and put them with a slap into Marlene's suddenly outstretched palm, which was as horny and calloused as any Hamburg docker's. 'All right, brother?'

'It'll do, brother. All right, you need the Soya-Bean Folk and the Duke of Moscow.' Marlene's voice grew softer. 'But tell them that Marlene sent you. Now then, this is how you get there . . .'

'We have emigrated from a corrupt society,' said the tall, emaciated, bespectacled civilian with the wisp of a beard round his receding chin, who had the look of an ex-schoolmaster about him. They clattered down the cellar which seemingly housed the strangely named group. 'We want neither their politics, their killings nor their food. Our substance we acquire from friends on the docks – sacks of soya-bean flour, very sustaining.' Schulze looked at One-Flipper significantly. Now they knew why they were called the Soya-Bean Folk. 'Our shelter we find here in this waste-land, symbolic of man's basic evil.'

'What kind of people make up your group?' One-Flipper asked their guide, who didn't seem in the least perturbed that he was dealing with three armed SS men.

'Lesbians, deserters, Bible students[1], freemasons, homosexuals, all those individuals which our corrupt society regards as abnormal, dangerous or subversive – and communists.'

Schulze's eyes hardened. He knew his communists; he had been one himself in his younger days on the Hamburg waterfront. They were the best organized and most efficient of all the groups now emerging as the opposition in a dying '1000-Year Reich'. 'Would the Duke of Moscow be a communist by any chance?' he asked.

Their guide smiled thinly, obviously amused by Schulze's naïvety. 'What else with that name, my friend?'

The guide paused at the bottom of the stairs and extended a dirty skinny hand at the packed room, obscured by cigarette smoke and giving off the stale sickly-sweet smell of soya beans, and pointed to a gross, brutal-looking man, a head taller than Schulze, who squatted on an upturned barrel in the far corner of the cellar, surrounded by women in various stages of undress. 'The Duke of Moscow, *meine Herren*.'

One-Flipper looked at Schulze. The big NCO shrugged, as if to say, 'What have we got to lose?' and started to push his way through the excited throng, who sounded and looked as if their diet of soya beans was washed down with liberal quantities of schnapps. A minute later he was facing the Duke of Moscow, whose red-clad belly hung obscenely over his trousers, the flies of which were open for very obvious reasons.

[1] The 10,000 Bible students were imprisoned in Nazi Germany because they refused to swear an oath of allegiance to Hitler.

He took an instant dislike to the gigantic communist with his cropped bullet-head and mouthful of blackened teeth, but there was no way back now. 'Heil Moscow!' he rapped challengingly and grinned at the other man.

The girl who had been fumbling in the Duke's flies took her hand away, as if she had just been stung, and glared at the SS man. Slowly, very slowly, the Duke deigned to become aware of the SS man. 'Since when did we steal horses together, friend?' he asked in a low voice full of menace. Poking a forefinger like a small sausage at his massive chest, he said, 'See this shirt, friend?' Schulze nodded. 'You recognize the colour?' Again Schulze nodded, but said nothing. 'Well, I'm gonna tell you, friend, where that red colour came from to dye this shirt.'

'Tell me,' Schulze said challengingly. 'Don't make me wait in suspense.'

The irony seemed wasted on the Duke of Moscow. 'It came from the blood of the Nazis' skulls I've cracked in my time.' He brought his massive fists together, as if smashing a head between them, and the girl who had been playing with him dodged back in alarm. 'That shirt bears the blood of one police president, at least two police lieutenants and the Gauleiter of Hamburg himself.'

'Don't say any more,' Schulze said in a high-pitched affected voice, 'or I'll cream my skivvies. You see, Duke, I'm very delicate and get the dry heaves at the very thought of blood.'

The Duke of Moscow glared at him. 'You're risking a fat lip, friend,' he threatened. 'There are only three of you, you know.'

Schulze remained unmoved.

'What are you SS pigs doing here anyway?' the Duke of Moscow asked. 'You wanting to bugger off now that your beloved Führer is getting his arse kicked in the east, eh? Is that what you're here to see the Duke for?'

Slowly, very slowly, Schulze opened his palm to reveal his last diamond.

The Duke of Moscow narrowed his pig-like eyes at the

sight and whistled softly. 'That looks like the real thing,' he said after a while.

'It is,' Schulze answered, and with a careless gesture tossed it into the Duke's wide-open flies.

Hastily the girl retrieved it and handed it to an eager Duke, who stared at it carefully, turning it in his massive paws many times, as if he couldn't see enough of it. 'I think you're right,' he said finally, '*and?*'

'And – it's yours!'

'For what?'

Schulze hesitated and looked around the now-silent room. There were too many people present for his liking. How did he know that there might not be a Gestapo spy among them? 'Get rid of this bunch of perverted banana suckers and I'll tell you.' He grinned for the first time since he had entered the Soya-Bean Folk's cellar. 'Let's see a bit of that ducal muscle, eh?'

FIVE

'I don't trust the big bastard,' Matz said firmly, looking at the other two in the flickering yellow light of the candle, the only illumination in the cellar, which the Soya-Bean Folk had allotted to the Wotan men.

'Do you think I want to go to bed with the Red swine?' Schulze growled, and shoved his cap to the back of his cropped head in exasperation.

'Yes,' One-Flipper said carefully. 'His manner was too unconcerned. He gave us the information we wanted to know, yet he didn't ask one single question. Why? He's no fool, in spite of his foul manners. Of all people, he would be the one who should be interested in why we need info about the Neuengamme CC. He hasn't survived twelve years in the Commie underground without having kept his eyes and ears open.'

'Agreed, sir,' Schulze replied. 'Let's understand right from the start that the Duke of Moscow's gonna give us the purple shaft just as soon as it suits his shitting purpose. All right?'

The other two nodded their agreement.

'Good, now I'm gonna work out something soon to fix the Duke of Moscow's heels for him. I've got a couple of the boys watching that cellar as it is. But for the time being, let's see what we got out of the big bastard. One – ' Schulze ticked off the point with his thick finger – 'Neuengamme is very heavily guarded. It's too near Hamburg and these illegals for them to allow prisoners to escape. Two, most of the guards are older fellers who live off camp with their families. Three, the hospital in which your wife works is in the outer camp. Fourth, both the inner camp, which is not our concern, and the outer one, which is, are under the control of the Commie *Kapos*.[1] Fifth, the *Kapos* are only

equivalent to an English 'trusty', who were responsible for the internal running of the camps.

interested in the survival of their fellow commies. The rest, the Yids, the warm brothers and the like, can go up the chimney all the time.' Schulze made the gesture of smoke rising from the concentration-camp ovens. 'It's no skin off their noses. Sixth, though the Duke of Moscow didn't tell us this, those *Kapos* don't want the boat rocked in any way. They're gonna survive the war come what may, and they don't want to have their eggs shot off at this stage of the game for anybody. So what have we got?'

'I'll tell you, Schulzi,' Matz said cynically. 'Not only will the screws at Neuengamme be after our arses, the Duke of Moscow will be too – *and* his shitting *Kapos*.'

'Exactly, my little crippled friend,' Schulze said and let the information sink in.

'But at the moment, Schulze,' One-Flipper said, 'the Duke of Moscow doesn't know *why* we need this information. So that gives us a slight edge over him.'

'For a bit anyway, sir. But we can't afford to sit around

[1] *Kapos*, heads of sections in concentration camps, roughly

for ever on our butts, playing with our dongs. We've got to get this thing on the road – and quick!'

'What do you suggest?'

Schulze grinned. 'Well, of course, you officers and gents are paid to think; us common foot-folk, we just take orders like the peasants we are.'

One-Flipper returned the grin. 'Get on with it, you big rogue. You could lose and find many a General-Staff officer with the crimson stripe down his breeches.'

'All right, sir, this is what I've been thinking. The guards at Neuengamme work normal civvies' shifts, morning, afternoon and night, eight hours on, sixteen hours off. Each shift is divided into two groups, twenty men to guard the inner camp and ten for the outer. If . . .'

'I can see how your mind's working, Schulze,' One-Flipper interrupted excitedly. 'The night shift . . . and the outer guard?'

'Exactly, sir. With a bit of luck, we've got the hospital staff asleep in the building in the outer camp and hopefully those Bolshy *Kapos* in the hay too, sawing wood. And, of course, it will be dark.'

Matz bit his bottom lips thoughtfully. 'You mean, we're gonna take over the night shift?'

'You've got it, bird-brain.'

'But we can't just march up there and wait outside the gate until they come on duty and say nice and polite, hand over yer uniform, brother, 'cos we want to carve out one of your prisoners. Come off it, Schulzi, you must haven't all yer cups in yer cupboard to think it's gonna be that simple!' He glowered scornfully at the other man.

Schulze was not put out. 'They come in in two shifts, by truck, the outer guard shift arriving exactly five minutes after the inner shift. According to the Duke of Moscow, it's something to do with the camp's standing orders, so that there's always somebody on duty during the change of shifts. And we, ape-turd, are gonna to borrow that second truck. Get it?'

'Got it!'

'You're forgetting one thing,' One-Flipper said after a few moments of silence. 'There's still the Duke of Moscow to be dealt with, and God knows how many commies there are running around in the Dead Zone to protect him!'

For what seemed an eternity, Schulze did not reply, then as the first thin wail of the sirens started to drift into the cellar to indicate that Hamburg's nightly air-raid was about to commence, he grinned and rose to his feet, carefully slipping the 'Hamburger Equalizer' over his big hand. 'Thank God for the buck-teethed, knock-eyed Tommies, you can at least rely on them to be on time.'

'But where are you going?' both Matz and One-Flipper cried in unison.

'To pay my loyal respects to the Duke of Moscow, of course,' Schulze replied easily. 'Where else?' And with that he was gone . . .

'The world, the whole world, will swing to the Left,' the bearded Soya-Bean Folk leader was declaiming, his weak face flushed with emotion. 'Except, that is, America. Everyone will be happy, alert, healthy.' He threw out his skinny arm in a spacious gesture as if to embrace the world. 'There will be abuses, of course. Unfortunately there will be those unenlightened people who will still want to eat meat. But I suppose one can never expect to have a perfect society.'

The Duke of Moscow gazed at him with undisguised contempt and pushed the girl's head down closer to his loins; he was beginning to enjoy her attentions, although these Soya-Bean women weren't as good as the professional pavement-pounders he usually serviced.

'Of course, after the "1000-Year Reich" has finally vanished, there will be other organizations that must be taken care of. The Catholic Church, for instance, the military, the . . .'

His words died away as the whistle outside grew suddenly shriller and shriller by the instant. His face blanched. '*A bomb!*' Everybody hit the floor as the clattering screaming noise grew into a terrible, ear-splitting intensity, like an express train racing down the track at full speed.

The explosion rocked the deep cellar. The floor heaved alarmingly. Somewhere windows blew out. The candles flickered wildly, throwing grotesque huge waving shadows on the trembling walls. The explosion seemed to rumble on and on for ever, but diminishing in sound so that from outside they could hear the slither of falling masonry and the tumbling of many bricks. Finally, a blast of hot acrid air shot down the cellar steps and it was all over, leaving them coughing and choking and beating the white dust off their clothing.

'More?' the Soya-Bean woman demanded, still on her knees, her blouse open to reveal her skinny yellow breasts.

The Duke looked down at his open flies and saw that the sudden explosion had caused all desire to die. 'Ner,' he snorted, angry with her and the bomb that had spoilt his pleasure, 'you couldn't even suck a lollipop!'

The Soya-Bean woman started to cry. The Duke of Moscow ignored her. Tucking in his blood-red shirt, 'stained with the life-juices of a hundred Nazis', as he always liked to boast to his cronies, he indicated that he was leaving. Immediately his bodyguard fell in and began to march up the stairs, now littered with rubble, as if they were escorting a real duke.

Outside in the blacked-out darkness there was a sullen smell of explosive smoke in the night air. Somewhere closer to the heart of the bomb-shattered port, scarlet flames leapt into the sky and their reflection quivered in the broken glass that lay everywhere in the cobbled street. Water gurgled somewhere from a burst water-main.

The Duke of Moscow ignored the smells and sound; he knew them only too well from the last two years of 'terror bombing', as that crippled little poison-dwarf Goebbels called the Anglo-American Imperialists' raids.

His heavy boots crunched over the glass, while his bodyguard spread out on both sides of the Duke, eyes alert, weapons in their hands. The Duke sucked his rotten, blackened front teeth and tried to figure out what the game of the SS men was. What would they want in Neuengamme? If they were deserters, why would they want to know about a C-Camp? And there was an officer with them too. Even with war in its present state of collapse, he had never heard of one of *their* officers deserting. He frowned. Could he do a deal with Kauffmann, the Nazi *Gauleiter* of Hamburg? He knew from his Party contacts in Denmark and Sweden that the *Gauleiter* was shitting himself and was trying to do a deal with the Anglo-American Imperialists via the Swedes. Kauffmann might well be interested in doing some business with Hamburg's illegal CP cell in return for a bunch of SS men, who were obviously up to no good. It was an angle anyway.

They passed a small car which had been hit by the bomb blast. It lay against a wall, crushed and compressed by the explosion as if it had been put through a giant baling machine, its driver flattened to a pancake behind the wheel.

The sight amused the Duke. 'Hey, you lot,' he called, 'come over here and have a look-see at this! There's a stiff here pressed as flat as an ox-tongue.'

His bodyguard crowded around him and thus missed the movements in the rubble around them.

'Shit,' the Duke of Moscow said. 'You know it's a pity you couldn't dry something like that and keep it. It'd look good on a wall as a kind of decoration . . . Like that tobacco pouch made out of a Popov's ball-race that old Hans brought back from the Eastern Front. Mind you,' he added hastily with a grin, 'old Hans did say that the Popov he cut it off'n from wasn't a member of the Party.' His bodyguard laughed dutifully at their boss's jokes.

Over near the Alster, Hamburg's internal lake, the flak was belting away and the group craned their heads to look at the fireballs exploding above their heads, while the searchlights parted the clouds with cold silver fingers looking for the Tommy intruders who had now spent two years slaughtering this city.

A plane appeared, silver and tiny, spreadeagled against the sky like some strange metallic insect pinned on a card in a museum, trapped on all sides by the searchlights.

In the same instant that the flak zeroed in on the trapped Lancaster and it exploded in a violent searing flash of crimson, the gleaming silver pieces of metal bursting outwards like a starshell, a hard challenging voice called, 'Well, Duke, how does it feel now to be mixing with the common-folk, eh?' The bodyguards swung round, hands dropping to their concealed weapons. Too late! In the blood-red light of the falling plane, a circle of stark black silhouettes were revealed standing there, weapons levelled.

'Freeze those little pinkies of yours where they are, gents, and no harm'll come to you,' Schulze ordered and, with surprising lightness for such a big man, dropped to the road in front of the Duke of Moscow.

'Oh, it's you, eh. I thought you bastards of the SS were up to no good. Now I know it,' the Duke said without any apparent fear. He exposed his big teeth in the kind of a grin that made a man like Schulze aggravated, more especially when he breathed the fetid odour that came from the communist's mouth.

'Christ, when did you last brush your choppers?' he snarled. 'Before the war?'

'Could be,' the Duke said easily.

A silent alarm went off in Schulze's brain. The Red bastard was too confident. Here he was, trapped in a Dead Zone backstreet with five machine pistols pointing in his direction, yet he was showing no sign of fear. Indeed the situation might have been reversed with the Duke having all the cards in his hands. Why?

'You're pretty cocky for a fella who might well be looking at the taties from below in a few minutes time?' he said, trying to make his voice sound casual.

'I've been around. SS pigs like you, however big they are, don't make the Duke of Moscow cream his skivvies, you know. I've had your size and bigger for breakfast before today.'

'You're risking getting a fat lip, comrade,' Schulze said and tentatively thrust his fist against the Duke's massive chest.

The communist did not even budge. He reached up a big paw and scratched his unshaven jaw, making a sound like sandpaper being rasped against wood. 'Be careful, soldier boy, you'll make me have my monthlies in a minute, out of sheer fright.' He guffawed coarsely.

It had originally been Schulze's plan to beat the Duke into insensibility and then give the Wotan men a chance to leave the Dead Zone without hindrance. Minus their *Kapo*, his bodyguard could not think. Now he knew he had to somehow get out of the big communist what he was holding back, or risk their plans being sabotaged. But how could he break him down? Threats would have no effect upon him. The Duke knew his reputation rested on fear and that he dare not be intimidated in front of his bodyguard.

'Do you know – you're a fat-gutted, blow-hard shit, Duke?' he tried in an almost conversational tone. 'It's my guess that you've been cowering in some damned cellar for most of the war, while the real men went to war, and have only emerged now that there's no danger to yourself. Besides, ain't you got your bully-boys here to do your fighting for you?'

'What do you mean?' the Duke growled, iron suddenly in his deep voice.

'You heard me, or have you been eating big beans again?'

'Schulze, you've got a loose tongue, you know.'

'Yeah, and I think you've got a loose gut. Better watch it and don't open yer asshole too wide or there might be an unfortunate accident. Did you hear that, boys?' Schulze raised his voice. 'The Duke here might shit his ducal britches.'

Dutifully the men with the machine pistols guarding the civilians laughed.

'You looking for a knuckle-sandwich?' the Duke growled dangerously.

'Are you trying to pull my pisser? A knuckle-sandwich

from a fat-gutted blowhard like you,' Schulze answered. 'Don't make me laugh!'

The Duke of Moscow flexed his arms and fingers and, in the light of the searchlights, Schulze could see the look in his eyes. It was dangerous; he was getting ready to charge. Carefully, like a dentist about to make an extraction and hiding his pincers at the side of his body in order not to frighten his patient, he held the 'Hamburger Equalizer' at the ready. It wasn't fair, but nothing was fair in war.

The Duke's breath came in fast jets. Suddenly he lunged at Schulze. The latter dodged the blow easily by simply swaying to one side and not even moving his feet.

He laughed. 'Pretty piss-poor, Duke. Think you'll have to do better.'

The Duke launched a tremendous kick at his shin. Schulze side-stepped and, catching the other man off balance, stamped down hard on his other foot. As the Duke howled and hopped around, clutching his injured foot, Schulze kicked him in the face. He shot backwards, spitting out teeth everywhere.

Now Schulze gave him no more chances. He strode forward to where the Duke now crouched on his hands and knees in the dirty slush of the gutter, shaking his head to clear the blood that clogged his nose and ruined mouth, glaring up at his opponent with little red pig-like eyes that were already beginning to turn violet and green. 'Don't think . . . you . . . scare . . . me,' he sobbed, spitting out blood with every laboured word. 'Because you – '

With one immense, downward movement and a huge grunt, Schulze reached and hauled the groggy Duke to his feet. He pulled back the fist to reveal the gleaming brass knuckles for the first time, seeing the Duke's eyes narrow with abject terror as he saw them, and smashed it into the Duke's fat chest, making a sound like a mallet wrapped in a wet cloth.

The Duke howled. Schulze showed no mercy. Systematically he pounded the big communist, blood spraying from beneath the Hamburger Equalizer each time he hit him, ignoring the other man's screams of agony and pleas for mercy. Time and time again until the blood ran in scarlet streams down the Duke's upper lip, making Schulze's other hand so greasy that he could hold the limp bulk of the Duke no longer.

He let him drop into the slush and towered over him, his own chest heaving frantically, his breath coming in sharp, noisy gasps like those made by an ancient holed leather bellows. For one long moment, outlined by the cold merciless light of the silver beams, they faced each other like that, the classic picture of victory and utter defeat, and then Schulze pulled himself together. Slipping off his brass knuckles, knowing that he would not need them now, he grabbed hold of the Duke's long, greasy hair and pulled that mangled pulped face close to his own, trying to ignore the stench of sweat, fat and bloody fear which assailed his nostrils. 'Listen, bigshot, I want to know what kind of nasty plans you have for us,' he barked.

The Duke shook his head, seemingly unable to speak. Schulze tapped him lightly across the face like a girl might tap her lover playfully for having been too forward.

The Duke screamed high and hysterical.

'Shit on the shingle!' one of his bodyguards exclaimed in disgust and, in spite of the machine pistols still levelled at him and the others, turned away as if he could not bear to view such craven cowardice any longer. Schulze instinctively knew that the big communist's days were over in the Dead Zone; he had lost face for good. But at the moment other things concerned him. 'I asked you a question, you fat bubbler barrel, and I want an answer. Or do you want another dose of what you've just had?' He drew back his fist as if about to smash it once more into that red gore that was the Duke's face.

'No . . . no . . .' the Duke screamed. 'NO!'

'All right then, pee or get off the pot. What have you done?'

In blood-thickened and almost unintelligible words, the fallen man spelt out what he had intended to do; how he had thought of approaching Hamburg's *Gauleiter* with what he had found out about these strange SS men who had appeared so mysteriously in the Dead Zone, but had not done so.

'Is that all?' Schulze demanded when the long-drawn, blood-thickened account was finished. 'Come on, out with it, fat guts. Or else . . .'

'There's one other thing.'

'Yes?'

'I got word to the Artist to keep his eye open for you,' the Duke forced out the words with an effort of sheer will-power, spitting blood the whole time.

'The Artist?'

'Chief *Kapo* in the . . . the hospital.'

'And is that all?' Schulze demanded, tugging at the Duke's long hair cruelly, forcing him to open his eyes that were violet, juffed, and virtually closed now.

'I swear it . . . Honest . . .'

With an expression of disgust Schulze let go of the man. His head fell to the dirty cobbles with an audible thud. He turned to the bodyguards, while behind him in the gutter the beaten communist started to sob like a broken-hearted little child, his fat shoulders heaving. 'All right, my Red friends, you'd better sod off and find yourselves some new royalty. The Duke of Moscow has just gone and abdicated . . .'

He spat contemptuously in the slush next to the sobbing man and turned without another look at him or his bodyguards. Now he knew all he needed to know.

Five

Neuengamme

ONE

It looked very ordinary. Not bad at all. A couple of kilometres from the Elbe village of Neuengamme, set off a rutted farm track that apparently led to nowhere, it could have been just another *Wehrmacht* camp, of the kind that had sprung up everywhere in the rural areas since 1939.

There was the usual collection of dark-brown wooden one-storey huts, grouped around what could have been a parade ground, in the centre of which the usual swastika flag fluttered proudly or limply depending on the state of the wind. There was the normal two-metre-high double barbed-wire fence about which soldiers might have joked that it was there not to keep them from getting out illegally but to keep the sex-starved local women from getting in. But the stork-legged watchtowers, manned by steel-helmeted guards armed with the MG 42, seemed out of place. That was not the only thing that told the uninformed passer-by, of which there were few from the local area (even the Elbe farmers avoided the camp like the plague), that there was something out of the ordinary about Neuengamme Camp. It was the smell.

The sweet sickly smell of gas that suffused the air for metres around and in summer turned the vegetation in the immediate area of the camp an unwholesome pale yellow. And the closer one got to the camp, the worse that stench of escaping gas got, mixed now with the odour of what could only be that of burning flesh, so that only the bravest could tolerate that noxious stench without retching and vomiting even before they reached the barbed-wire covered gate.

The survivors and the guards inside had got used to it, their nostrils somehow deadened to that terrible smell. But over the years that they had served in Neuengamme Concentration Camp, the middle-aged guards and the *Kapos*, with the coloured patch of the political prisoner on their striped pyjama-like uniform, had had to face much worse than the stench.

Daily they had been confronted with the staring, cavernous eyes of the victims, so far sunk in tragedy that their expression was no longer human, but animal. Daily they had lived with walking scarecrows, with pale-lipped, skull-like faces that already seemed to have suffered death long before. Daily they had ordered the piles of rags and bones that had once been human beings to be heaped up in great stacks like logs of wood ready for burning. And daily they bought their own lives for another precious twenty-four hours by taking the lives of others. This then was Neuengamme Concentration Camp *anno* 1945 in the last year of existence of Hitler's Reich, which he had once proclaimed would last a thousand years . . .

The Artist waited patiently until the SS *Oberscharführer* had unfolded the light brown object on the wooden-plank table in front of him, taking great care not to rip it or crease it more than it had been normally creased by nature. But the Artist had time. He had survived the Gestapo Interrogation Centre beneath the cellars of Berlin's Number 10 Prinz Albrecht Strasse; he had survived five years of Dachau and then two years of Copenhagen's lunatic asylum, when he had escaped and pretended to be crazy. Now he intended to survive the last few months in this hell-hole and receive his due rewards for nearly twelve years of unbroken service to the CP, two as an 'illegal' and ten years behind 'Swedish curtains'. Thus he waited until Wolfgang the *Oberscharführer*, whose love-life now centred around animals, after the years of perverted love-making in the camps, and whose artistic tastes ran to the bizarre, to put it mildly, was ready to explain his latest wish to him.

Dietz straightened up and looked at the pale-faced communist with the deceptively gentle eyes. 'Now, get this, Artist, I don't want those tattoos destroyed.' Indicating the usual boring snakes and crossed heart that decorated the skin, he continued, 'Came off a seaman – Dane or Norwegian, something like that, he couldn't speak in the end – who got them done overseas. So they're different – and I don't want 'em spoiled or it'll be the worst for you, you Red bastard.'

The Artist lowered his eyes, as if he were afraid. The contrary was the case. *Oberscharführer* Dietz thought he ran the inner camp, but in fact it was really he, the Artist, and his fellow *Kapos* who did. Already they had enough weapons hidden in the camp to deal with the ruptured old has-beens of the General SS who presently guarded them. Slowly he raised his gaze and looked at the sergeant, whose face looked as if it had been made of flaky cheese. 'I'll take every care, *Oberschar*,' he said humbly, 'as always. But what have you in mind for this piece?'

'A lampshade, I think,' Dietz remarked finally, after apparently giving the matter some thought. 'I've got a flower bowl covered in it. Remember that Jew with the dark skin – might have thought he was a nigger, he was that black? My personal diary is the same stuff. But of course you couldn't waste this kind of material on a diary or anything like that, could you?'

'Of course not,' the Artist agreed hastily, wondering how a man like Dietz, a former bricklayer, had got like this – dogs and lampshades made of human skins. 'Naturally I'll give it my whole attention.'

Dietz smiled, his yellow false teeth bulging uglily out of his pale, bloodless lips. 'Good. Do you know what, Artist?' he said with a sudden outburst of enthusiasm.

'No, *Oberschar*.'

'That big-titted Polack in the spital, the one whose bits and pieces have been scraped out by the bone-menders and is croaking it.' He made an expansive gesture with both his weak hands. 'God, what a pair of lungs she's got! Anyway, I've made a deal with one of the bone-menders that he's gonna give me one of her tits when she kicks off. He'll clean it up for me, of course,' he added hastily.

'Of course, *Oberschar*.'

'It'd make a terrific tobacco-pouch, you know. Imagine

the laugh you'd get with the boys in the mess, pulling that out and saying to no one in particular, "Anyone like a pipe-ful of Polack tit?"' He roared at his own humour, his flaky face seeming about to fall to bits at any moment. 'The boys'd piss themselves.'

'That they would indeed, *Oberschar*.'

Dietz's face grew suddenly serious. Through the dirty window he had glimpsed his personal *bête noire*: *shitting* Frau *shitting* Doktor *shitting* Irma *shitting* Flosse, head of the primitive hospital the commandant tolerated to attent to those Neuengamme inmates able to go out daily on the various work commandos and thus dodge the ovens. His gross features darkened. Why Himmler had personally ordered that nothing should happen to the woman, he would never know. She was a pain in the arse. Always playing the suffering lady in white, her whole existence devoted to the welfare of her miserable 'patients', even forgoing her own rations for their sakes, sometimes daring to talk back to him, *Oberscharführer* Wolfganf Dietz, who in his time had made strong men piss their pants with one casual look.

He nodded to the Artist. 'Here comes the God in white,' he said sarcastically. 'There's no need for her to see my – er – skin. Put it away, Artist, please.'

The Artist did as he was ordered, just as Dr Irma Flosse opened the door of the hospital and came in, her ragged coat clean and white in spite of the lack of soap, her eyes eager and cheerful, although below them there were the deep blue circles of undernourishment and exhaustion. 'Good morning, *Oberschar* . . . Good morning, Artist,' she said politely, but without warmth, as if she had summed them both up long before and found them, guard and prisoner, wanting. 'My orders for the day, *Oberscharführer*?'

Oberscharführer Heinz took his time, as befitted one of the masters, staring the doctor up and down from her bare, frozen feet in the home-made wooden clogs to her cropped blonde hair tied back tight against her head. 'You are to make a definite decision whether those three Danes of yours are fit for a work commando. Or else?' He made the old,

old gesture of smoke ascending.

The cheerful grin went from Dr Flosse's face. 'They'll be fit, *Oberschar*,' she promised hastily.

'And what's the situation with the female Polack? Find that out, too, and report her state to me, *personally*!' He poked a big thumb at his skinny weak chest. 'Got it?'

'Yes, *Oberschar*.'

'Good.' He picked up his whip and slapped it ineffectively against the side of his jackboot that enclosed his spindly leg. '*Morgen*.'

'*Morgen, Oberschar*,' both of them said dutifully.

The Artist grinned after his bent back. 'Exit the blond beast,' he sneered. 'The finest type of Aryan – the little perverted creep.'

'And you?' Dr Flosse asked, knowing instinctively what the parcel he held contained.

The Artist flushed, a rare occurrence with him after twelve years on the run or in prison. 'One has to survive,' he said dully.

'Has one?' she asked and then turned, walked the best she could in her wooden clogs towards the hospital. Another day in Neuengamme Concentration Camp had commenced.

TWO

Visibility was virtually zero. The wind howled down the narrow country road leading to the village of Neuengamme, whipping up the snow in frenzied dances so that the whirling flakes penetrated every gap in the waiting men's uniforms, lashed their crimson, frozen faces and clung to their boots in huge clumps.

But, blanketed as he was in an impenetrable icy cocoon of vicious white, one-Flipper was glad of the cover the sudden snowfall provided. Not only that, anyone coming down the road this night would be concentrating on keeping his vehicle on the abruptly slick and treacherous surface.

The thought of a hold-up would be the furthest from any driver's mind.

Twice the freezing Wotan men crouched in the ditches on both sides of the road were startled by false alarms. Once a great creaking farm-cart came lumbering down the road, towed by two huge oxen, great jets of steam coming from their nostrils, their massive heads lowered against the driving snowflakes, a farmer sat on the box, his head muffled in a potato-sack. Some time later a truck came groaning up the road in second gear and One-Flipper just restrained his tense, over-eager men in time. It crunched by, its open back packed with human skeletons dressed in what appeared to be striped pyjamas, heads bent in abject, complete defeat.

One-Flipper peered through the flying snow at Schulze. The latter nodded his head; he had seen them too. They were the inmates of Neuengamme. The victims. One-Flipper held his side, trying to stop the sudden physical pain there. Would his beloved Irma look like that too now?

Time passed in freezing leaden silence. More than once One-Flipper peered through the white gloom at his wrist-watch, mentally trying to force the green-glowing hands to move quickly. The first truck with the inner guard was scheduled to bring them on duty for six o'clock; the second for five minutes after six. Now it was almost six. What had happened? Had the snowfall affected the schedules somehow? Were they perhaps not going to make an appearance at all this terrible winter night? What if . . .

The questions died suddenly in some remote corner of his over-excited brain. Again there was the sound of a vehicle crawling up the road from Neuengamme in low gear. One-Flipper raised his head above the ditch. Next to him Schulze did the same. Twin slits of blue light were visible through the howling snowstorm. '*Wehrmacht* truck,' Schulze identified the typical military blackout immediately.

A minute later the truck crawled past them, its open back packed with armed men, blankets and sacks thrown over their heads to keep out the whirling snow, rifles clutched between their knees, crouched there in frozen misery.

'It's them,' One-Flipper hissed excitedly, as the truck went by. 'It has to be!' He flung a glance at the luminous dial of his wristwatch and checked the time. Five minutes from now.

Now they tensed. Next to Schulze, Matz crouched poised, with two sturdy Wotan men ready with the tree trunk behind him. Everyone cocked their ears to the wind, trying to be the first to catch the noise of the second truck. The wind howled. The snow beat through the night sky like frenzied flak. Behind them the great oaks swayed and creaked alarmingly. To Schulze, it seemed as if this might be the way the world might end. Time passed with obstinate, stubborn slowness. And then there was sound again. 'Army truck!' Matz identified it, his hearing keener than that of the rest. 'Could be it!'

One-Flipper knew it *had* to be the one. He took a chance. 'All right, Matz,' he hissed urgently. 'Set up the trap.'

'Move it,' Matz ordered his two helpers. 'Get some pepper in yer pants!' Grunting with effort, the two young men heaved the tree trunk and deposited it hastily into the snow on the road to the front of the ambush position, so that it looked as if the snow might well have brought it down.

One-Flipper picked up his black Malacca cane and straightened up. Schulze peered up at him. 'Sure you want to go through with this alone, sir?' he asked swiftly as the roar of the truck grew even louder.

'Quite sure, Schulze. We've got to stop that truck without trouble. You take care that none of the bastards in the back escape.'

'Will do, sir.'

The sound of an overworked motor in low gear was almost upon them now. One-Flipper stood next to the tree trunk, his breath coming in short hectic little gasps, as if he had just run a race. There was a crash of gears as the driver brought the vehicle down from second to first in order to take the bend some fifty metres away from their positions, and then the truck swung into sight, looking with its two slits of blue light like some fiery-eyed predatory monster. One-Flipper's heart leapt. In the open rear there were the white-covered shapes of some eight or ten men. It was the truck bearing the outer guard relief to the camp!

Almost at the very last moment, with the windscreen wipers working frantically from side to side to clear the thick clogging snow, the driver saw the fallen tree. He hit the brakes. Too hard! For one moment a frantic One-Flipper thought he was going to have the truck off the road, as it shivered violently, skidding from one side to the other, the driver fighting the wheel with all his skill, the men in the back suddenly galvanized into violent action as they were flung from their seats. He caught it in the end and the truck slid to a shaky stop, its steaming square radiator entangled in the branches of the fallen tree. The driver leaned his head on the big wheel and breathed out hard, while from the back came angry cries of protest and alarm.

One-Flipper knew it was time for him to do his act before the guards started to drop over the tail-gate. He walked forward and tapped the door to the driver's near-side with his cane. 'You nearly had it there, didn't you, driver?' he called above the howling wind.

The driver started up as if he had been stung. 'Is there anyone out there?' he cried in alarm.

'Yes, Father Christmas! Of course there is someone out here, you idiot!' One-Flipper hit the door harder. 'Open up and let's see what kind of wet-tail is driving this heap!'

The door squeaked open and a narrow knife of yellow light slid into the white darkness. One-Flipper caught a swift look of an ashen, middle-aged face above the field-grey uniform of a General SS man. 'Hey, what's the like of you, Armed SS, doing out – '

The driver did not finish his cry. One-Flipper pressed the catch. The knife slid out of the end of the Malacca. The driver screamed thinly and reeled back as that deadly blade penetrated his heart. He slammed back against the cab, black blood already beginning to trickle from the side of his stupidly open mouth.

'Move it,' One-Flipper heard Schulze bellow suddenly. 'And watch those shitting uniforms!'

One-Flipper leaned back against the side of the truck, all energy sapped from him, as if someone had opened a sudden tap and it had run away. They had done it. The first stage of the rescue operation had been completed.

Irma Flosse looked down at the dying Polish woman, who shared a straw-filled canvas mattress with two other women, both of them dying too.

She shook her head and wondered what kind of doctors they were, who could conduct experiments on living healthy human bodies of the kind that had been carried out on the Polish woman. She passed on down the gloomy ward with the wooden bunks piled three-beds high right up to the roof, stopping here and there to change a paper-bandage, or offer some words of comfort, all that she could give, in half a dozen European languages, telling herself as she did so that she wasn't a doctor but merely a grave-digger in a white uniform.

'Well?' the Artist asked after she had come out of the last ward, pencil and paper at the ready, waiting for her to give her evening report, the *Meldung*.

'Well,' she answered, wearily rubbing the bridge of her nose and opening and closing her eyes several times, as if she were trying to focus them this way. 'Well, what?'

'*Meldung!* The *Oberschar* always insists that the *Meldung* is in his office first thing in the morning so that he can report to the *Kommandant* the strength of the work commandos.'

Irma Flosse thought if she hesitated a moment, she would cry. Instead she forced herself to say, 'My God, Artist, you and the rest of the communist *Kapos* never give up, do you? You're always there, doing everything they say. Reporting on time, with *jawohl, Scharführer* and at your command, *Scharführer*! What does it all matter? . . . They'll kill us all in the end, you know, *Kapo* or not.' She gave a tired laugh. 'Artist, you might be a toady, but you're no fool. You are an educated man, a real artist.'

The Artist looked at his wooden clogs, as if he did not want to be reminded of that other life: Paris, the girls, the theories, the hopes, all that talk.

'Do you really think that when they lost the war – and they will, you know – that they'll leave our kind alive to testify against that brown pack? No,' she shook her head firmly. 'They're hoping to get away with it. But they can only do that if the evidence is destroyed, neatly swept underneath the carpet and forgotten – *and we're that nasty evidence!*'

'I don't agree,' the Artist said, and taking the clipboard with the figures from her hands, as if he wanted to get on with his job and not listen to her talk, which somehow made him uneasy. 'We'll survive if we're disciplined and don't cause them trouble. In the end they'll run and we'll be masters here, but only if we don't make them panic.' He looked at her pale, tired, pretty face as if seeing it for the very first time. 'Doctor,' he said firmly, 'the guards – the lot of them – are bundles of nerves, sick in the body and sick in the mind. These years in the camps have perverted each and every one of them, from the commandant downwards, in a way that I don't think even the Roman emperors were perverted. Absolute power, you know – '

'I know.'

'Well, men like that panic easily. It is the duty of those of us who want to survive to ensure that they *don't* panic! One short-circuit and the brown bastards'll be running around slaughtering everything that comes in front of their sights. We've got to control them.'

'It's a nice thought, Artist,' she answered easily and yawned. 'But I for one have long given up believing in fairy-tales. When my time comes, I'm going to fight the bastards tooth-and-nail. They're not going to take Irma Flosse to the ovens like a dumb animal. Good night, Artist.'

'*Gute Nacht, Frau Doktor*,' the Artist said humbly, reverting to his usual tame self, but watching her keenly as she swept down the dirty corridor and out of the door into the dormitory in which the women employed in the outer camp slept. He told himself that Irma Flosse needed watching; she spelled trouble, and with victory for the Party, and freedom and power within grasping distance, the last thing on earth he wanted now was trouble.

Now he was alone in the shabby dirty camp hospital. Outside the wind howled and slapped at the blacked-out windows. A loose shutter clattered back and forth. Somewhere a dying man groaned in his sleep, speaking in a tongue that the Artist could not understand, even if he had been interested – which he wasn't.

Carefully he pulled the knife which the *Oberschar* had given him for the job out the front of his shabby striped pants; he had concealed it between them and the layers of brown wrapping paper beneath which gave him extra warmth. He tested its blade with his thumb. It was razor-sharp. It would need to be for the job he had planned.

Taking off his wooden shoes so that he would not make a noise, he walked cautiously to the ward which housed the Polish woman, the soles of his bare feet cringing when they came in contact with the icy-cold floor. He came to the bunk she shared with the other women.

Years before in Paris he had sketched such women, tied together in what had been obscene perverted embraces, executing the drawings in a fair imitation of Otto Dix's most cynical style. But there was nothing sexual about the poses of these three dying women – one Pole, one Russian, one Jewess – just a kind of pathetic hopelessness. Their once-young bodies seemed to express the thought that they had never expected in their wildest dreams to die in this place and in this manner.

The Polack stirred and in spite of the starvation rations he could see that her breasts beneath the sacking shift were still plump, firm and high. No wonder the *Oberschar* wanted them for his perverted collection.

The Artist looked at that long, dingy room with the yellow light colouring the bodies a sickly hue, as if he were memorizing it for another and better time, then he placed one hand over the Polack's mouth. Almost before she was aware of it, he had begun sawing through her throat . . .

Slowly the truck, the noise it made in low gear deadened by

the whirling snow, ground to a halt in front of the red-and-white striped pole that barred any further progress. A dim blue light clicked on above the sentry box near the gate and a fat, huddled figure in a steel helmet and angle-length grey coat shuffled out of it, rifle slung over his shoulder carelessly, lantern raised at shoulder level. '*Wer da?*' he challenged routinely, the wind snatching the words out of his mouth and dissipating them.

'Friends!' One-Flipper cried against the howl of the wind, leaning his helmeted head out of the cab, 'Outer-Camp guard coming on shift!'

The sentry beckoned them forward with a wave of his lantern, keeping his head screwed down well inside his upturned collar so that the driving snowflakes could not penetrate his greatcoat. The truck ground on another few metres, the windscreen wipers clicking back and forth like the pendulum of a clock in a vain attempt to keep them clear of the snowflakes.

The sentry looked up at One-Flipper. 'Who're you?' he asked without interest or alarm. 'Ain't seen you before!'

'Just been posted from the front.'

The sentry absorbed the information slowly, his shoulders rapidly being covered by snow, and then perhaps remembering some half-forgotten duty regulations, he grunted, 'Better let me see your paybook, comrade.'

'Of course,' One-Flipper said immediately and made a show of fumbling inside his heavy greatcoat, ears straining to catch the sound of soft footsteps doubling round from the back of the truck.

He heard them. The sentry didn't – until it was too late. 'Hey,' he began, as the shadow detached itself from the bigger shadow cast by the truck. 'What's this lark – '

Schulze's Hamburger Equalizer flashed. There was the soft click of metal striking bone. The sentry's head shot backwards. His lantern tumbled from nerveless fingers, but Matz caught it before it hit the snow. A moment later, one of the Wotan men had replaced the unconscious sentry in the little red-and-white striped box and the truck was crawling into the silent blacked-out camp underneath that ironic cynical sign proclaiming 'WORK MAKES FREE'. They were in.

THREE

'Where in God's name have you shower of shit been?' the guard commander asked, as the door opened, bringing in flying snow and a huge huddled figure. 'The boys on the towers are screaming blue murder! Old Harold says his eggs are about to drop off, it's that shitting cold. What – ' the words died on the fat guard commander's mouth as the huge huddled figure flung back the blanket which covered his head, to reveal a face unknown to him. 'Hey, who are you?' he began and then changed his mind. His hand reached out for the phone on the desk in front of him.

Schulze was quicker. His bayonet flashed. The guard commander screamed high and hysterical as his outstretched hand was transfixed to the desk by the razor-sharp blade. Schulze didn't hesitate. 'All right, get in here – *quick!*' he called outside.

The men waiting there needed no urging. The storm was getting ever worse with the snowflakes hissing through the air in stinging white pellets that filled the air so thickly that the men were left gasping for breath. They stumbled inside the guardroom, which smelt of stale smoke and sweat, shivering with cold, beating their clothes and stamping their boots to remove the snow heaped there.

'What now?' Matz asked, eyeing the guard commander who squatted there, fat face contorted with pain and covered in sweat, as if a thick grease had been applied to his cheeks.

'Will he co-operate?' One-Flipper joined in, surveying the guard as if he were a creature from another world.

'Oh, he'll co-operate all right,' Schulze said and with a grunt he withdrew the bayonet.

The man screamed as the blood started to jet in a scarlet stream from his ruined hand.

'Shut it up, you fat bastard, and listen to what I want you to do.' He raised the bloodstained bayonet again and the threat had its effect.

'Yes . . . yes . . . anything . . . but not that, *please*,' the guard commander quavered, eyes in the yellow light, wild with almost unreasoning fear.

'All right, now listen – and listen carefully. I want you to order the men out there to begin the usual guard change. Normal procedure. One by one they are to leave their towers, and come down here to sign off personally. Understand?'

'Yes, I understand . . . one by one . . . normal procedure . . . Sign off personally,' the wounded man replied in hasty, scared gasps. 'You'll have my full co-operation, I can assure you . . . full – ' The words died on his lips, as Schulze pointed the red-tipped bayonet straight at his eyes.

'You'd better, you fat slop, because if you slip up, it wouldn't be yer flipper this time . . . it'll be those glassy orbits of yours. Now get on with it!'

One by one the men on the tower, frozen and covered in snow, fought their way through the storm, bodies bent double, across the parade ground into the guardroom, forcing open the door, with more often than not a curse or a complaint on their blue lips, to be confronted, not with Sergeant Fleps, but with a room crowded with heavily-armed strangers. And one by one they were disarmed neatly by the man standing hidden by the door, even before they had recovered from their initial surprise.

By six-thirty, Wotan had all ten safely in their custody and were ready to proceed to stage two of the daring operation.

The Artist was almost finished with his ghastly job. Next to the dead Polack woman, the other two women stirred occasionally as he carefully sawed away at the second breast, but they were too far gone on their last journey to worry him. As for the rest of the sick in that ward, if they were conscious, they knew better than to interfere in whatever was happening below. Neuengamme Concentration Camp was no place for Christian fellow-love.

It took his ears some time to note the unusual noise coming from outside. The storm was raging as before, yet there was another sound that somehow should not be there at this time, now that the camp had settled down for another miserable freezing night. At first he thought that it might be some of his fellow *Kapos* of the outer camp, drunk on illicit potato or turnip schnapps, coming over to the hospital to find women. But his subconscious dismissed that thought. No one in his right mind, however sexually aroused, would venture out on such a terrible night. Who could it be?

He completed his task at last and carefully stored the two breasts in a piece of rag, slipping them inside his jacket, feeling their warmth against his skinny sunken chest and being oddly affected by the sensation, before walking softly to the nearest window.

He eased away the blackout. He was careful not to reveal any light. Up in the towers the guards would be angry to be on duty on a filthy night like this; they would be only too glad of any opportunity to let off steam, and he didn't want a burst of machine-gun slugs in his chest on account of his curiosity.

For a moment or two he could make out nothing, save the whirling snowflakes and stark, stork-legged silhouettes of the guard towers, from which regularly at five-minute intervals the twin searchlights swept the courtyard below in vain. He blinked his eyes several times and told himself that he must be imagining things. The night shift had just gone on duty. The sentries in the towers wouldn't be relieved yet for another two hours. And then he saw them, dark shapes pressed against the far wall, unseen by the men in the towers but revealed to him from his observation post opposite in the flash of silver light as it cut through the storm momentarily.

The Artist let the blackout drop back in place hurriedly and leant against the wall, his heart beating rapidly, his breath coming suddenly in short alarmed gasps. The men outside were dressed in uniforms, complete with weapons and steel helmets. So why were they hiding from their comrades in the towers of the inner guard? What was going on?

Abruptly he remembered the Duke of Moscow's warning which had come in via the grapevine, transmitted by the farmer from outside who came in to clean the latrines with his 'honey-dew cart', as the *Kapos* called the evil-smelling, barrel-like contraption with which he transported the human manure for his fields. He was to watch out for some Armed SS thugs, who were interested in the hospital. They could cause trouble and the CP wanted no trouble now when there was a good chance that in the chaos of the months to come, Hamburg would fall into their laps like an over-ripe plum. The Artist bit his bottom lip, feeling the wet warmth of the severed breasts drip against his stomach. What was he to do?

He chanced another peep out of the window. The dark figures pressed against the wall below had gone. The search-lights sweep left and right revealing nothing. Had he seen them? Or had it been a trick of the storm, a figment of his imagination, triggered off by the macabre little operation which he had just performed? For a moment he wondered fearfully if he were going crazy too, like all of them did if they managed to survive the camps long enough, even the guards such as *Oberscharführer* Dietz.

Of course, *Dietz*! He must report it to Deitz in the inner camp. He was the senior *Kapo* and he and his fellow communists would be in the shit if anything went wrong in the outer camp. His jaw tightened, his mind made up; he'd tell Dietz.

Hurriedly he walked to the end of the ward to the little office, which contained the pathetic medical supplies available to Dr Flosse and the duty telephone. It was locked. He knew that in advance. But locks didn't worry the Artist. He and his fellow *Kapos* had skeleton keys to all the locks in Neuengamme – if they had wanted to, they could have opened the Commandant's own safe. He slipped in the skeleton key and opened the door without difficulty. He wrinkled his nose at the smell of ether and walked over to the telephone. Without turning on the desk light and revealing his presence there to anyone who might be watching, he dialled Dietz's number. The numbers were secret and limited to the guards, but again the *Kapos* knew them; it wouldn't be the first time that they had used their knowledge to call through to the illegal CP headquarters in Berlin.

'Dietz,' a sleepy grumpy voice said at the other end.

'*Oberschar*, here's the Artist.'

Ditz woke up properly with an audible gulp of air. 'What did you say?' he roared. '*The Artist?* How in three devils' name did you get my number?'

'Don't worry about that now, *Oberschar*,' the Artist hissed urgently. 'Listen to this. There is something funny going on . . .'

'What do you mean – something funny?' Dietz growled.

The Artist ignored the question. 'In the outer camp just outside the hospital. If I were you, I'd get my digit out of the orifice and have a look-see at it.'

'*Was erlaubst du dir, du Scheissarsch* – ' Dietz began, but the Artist was not fated to hear the rest of the SS NCO's enraged outburst. Suddenly the telephone went dead in his hand and he knew instinctively that not only had the line been cut, but that his suspicions had been correct. There *was* trouble brewing.

FOUR

'*No . . . no, it can't be?*'

Sergeant-Major Schulze was not normally a sentimental man, but that cry wrenched at his very heart. He stared at the skinny woman with the mass of blonde hair at the end of the dimly-lit corridor through eyes that were suddenly blurred by tears.

Next to him, One-Flipper hobbled forward on his cane, one arm outstretched, to fling himself into the two arms awaiting him, while all around in the suddenly illuminated ward, there was the slow lift of burning, over-large luminous eyes and languidly waved hands clad in what looked like striped pyjamas. At the end of the left row of tiered bunks, a figure fell to the dirty floor and started a slow advance on hands and knees through the stinking gloom, croaking something in a foreign tongue at the awed, almost frightened men standing there at the entrance to the hospital. He had just about reached Schulze, groping fervently for his snow-covered boots, when he fell dead, his skeletal hand still outstretched.

Schulze gulped and whispered, 'My God in Heaven!'

Matz crossed himself instinctively in a gesture he had thought he had forgotten these many years.

Schulze's brain raced. He had seen much death in these last years, death in all his hideous variations, but never anything like this: a kind of living death, not imposed on the victims in the heat of battle, on with the heart full of rage and hatred, but coldly and calculatingly. This was organized death, stamped, sealed and signed from behind some office desk by some mild-mannered official, who loved his children and probably sang carols with them around the fir tree on Christmas Eve. And it was the more terrible because of it. He took his eyes off the skeletons stirring on all sides on the bunks with infinite, painful slowness and called, 'Sir, time's a-passing, we've got to get out of here!'

One-Flipper released himself from his wife's grip. 'At the double, Sergeant-Major,' he called back. 'Come on, Irma!' Hurriedly he guided his wife, her cheeks stained and wet with tears, towards the waiting men, their shoulders heavy with snow. 'Irma, this big rogue here, Schulze, is the one you can thank for your rescue.'

An oddly embarrassed Schulze took the proffered hand and muttered something about it not having been difficult and then turning, ignoring the hoarse croaks on all sides, started to lead the party the way it had come.

Matz opened the door to the courtyard. Everything seemed normal. The twin searchlights swung back and forth as before in a vain attempt to cut through the swirling white fog. Otherwise the tall wooden guard towers showed no sign of life. 'All clear,' he whispered.

One-Flipper nodded to Schulze. 'Take over the van, Sergeant-Major, I'll bring up the rear.'

One by one the first half of the Wotan slipped out into the howling storm and, veterans that they were, immediately took up their crouched positions against the wall in order to cover the next group.

Schulze dropped next to Matz, Schmeisser machine pistol at the ready, narrowed eyes trying to penetrate the white gloom.

'What's up?' Matz asked anxiously.

'The sky's up.'

'Come off it, you big plush-eared bastard,' Matz hissed. 'I can tell you're crapping yourself.'

'It's too easy,' Schulze growled uneasily. 'Too sodding-well easy! And when it's easy like this, it always goes wrong.'

'Christ, why don't you go and join the old women's knitting club?' Matz replied. 'All those old maids see shadows where there ain't any. We just struck it luck . . .'

The words died on his lips.

The flare hissed through the flying snow, cracked, exploded and hung there, bathing the outer courtyard in its startling blood-red light and freezing the men down there in fearful anticipation. But not for long.

'There they are!' a harsh voice yelled above the roar of the storm.

The hard silver beam of a searchlight cut the whirling white gloom, pinning the van against the wall where they crouched, making them feel as if they had just been discovered naked in the main street of Berlin.

Schulze caught a glimpse of dark figures on the rampart of the tower to his right, then almost immediately a slow ancient machine gun started to chatter. Glass shattered above his head. To his right a Wotan man screamed shrilly as a burst ripped open his guts and he fell gurgling thickly into the snow to die there, choked in his own blood.

He reacted instinctively. Pulling the stick grenade from his boot, he had yanked out the cord and thrown it in a single movement. It sailed through the air and struck the base of the tower. One stork-like leg gave. Suddenly the tracer was missing its target as the tower, groaning and creaking like a live thing submitted to intolerable pressure, started to collapse.

Schulze did not even wait for the tower to crash to the ground. He sprang to his feet, ignoring the tracer stitching into the snow with a vicious red-hot hiss a mere metre away, and yelled, 'At the double, Wotan . . . *At the double!*'

Abruptly the night was hideous with noise. The tower crashed to the ground in a great rending splintering of wood. Tracer hurried a fiery-red back and forth. Someone screamed high and hysterical. The windscreen of the truck that they had hijacked shattered in a mess of glass. A siren began to howl. A small car swung out of the inner compound. Schulze fired from the hip. Its windscreen vanished in a crazy jigsaw of gleaming broken fragments. The frantic driver fought to keep control. He failed. A howl of brakes. The screech of protesting rubber. The car shimmied and slammed into the nearest barracks. Its occupants screamed with fear and began to spring in terror from the suddenly burst windows.

The Artist doubled the length of the wall. He must reach the inner camp! There he would be safe. As he ran, he kept his left hand pressed to his chest to keep the two Polack tits from falling out.

Like a blow from a gigantic fist, the slug struck him squarely in the small of the back. So great was the impact that he could not even shout with the tremendous pain of the blow. Instead he found himself sinking to the ground, his legs giving way beneath him weakly and beyond his control. His last sight was that of the two blood-red breasts slipping from beneath his jacket and dropping to the suddenly red-stained snow, nipples upwards, so that they looked up at him like two accusing eyes.

Schulze ran towards the outer gate. He skidded to a stop just in time. A group of men were running heavily through the blinding snow towards it, barring any further progress. He dropped to one knee and gave them a quick, wild burst. A fat man screamed, his hands fanning the air wildly, and went down face-first. The others followed suit. Someone yelled an order. A ragged burst of fire winged its way in his direction. Schulze easily dodged it. 'Bollocks!' he gasped, spitting out snow as he dived for the cover of the nearest wall. 'Bollocks all the way!'

Matz skidded to a stop next to him, bullets stitching a vicious pattern at his heels. 'What's up?' he gasped.

'Everything's up!' Schulze cried, beside himself with rage. Suddenly their whole plan had gone wrong. 'Watch in the bucket, VD in the heart.'

'You mean we can't get out by the main gate?'

'You said it, you crummy little arse with ears,' Schulze moaned.

'What we gonna to do?'

'What do you think . . .' the rest of Schulze's angry retort was drowned by the chatter of a heavy machine gun, which told him the guards had managed to bring one into position next to the main sentry-box. Now the gate was definitely out of the question. 'Back off,' he commanded, making up his mind in an instant. 'Back off and pass the word on to the Lieutenant.'

'But – '

'No sodding buts! Just do as I say. I'll keep these shits busy for a couple of minutes till One-Flipper has thought of some other way out of this shitting mess. *Now beat it, Matz!*'

Matz waited no longer. As Schulze thrust his machine pistol round the corner and fired a wild burst to cover his retreat, he pelted the best he could with his artificial leg back to where the rest of the Wotan crouched in the cover of a low stone wall, returning the fire of the guards in the towers of the inner camp.

Quickly he told an anxious One-Flipper about the situation at the main gate, and how Schulze thought there was no chance of their getting out now that way.

One-Flipper groaned out loud. 'Heaven, arse and cloudburst!' he cursed angrily. 'And I thought we'd pulled it off nicely, without any trouble.' He slammed the snow with his cane. '*Shit, shit . . . shit . . .*'

Matz had no patience with his outbursts. He knew there was not a moment to be lost. 'Sir, we've got to make a decision. You can bet yer bottom dollar that they've already alerted Hamburg or the nearest police post. They'll already be on their way. We've got to make dust – *and soon!*'

'But how, man?' One-Flipper cried in despair. '*HOW?*'

'I know,' his wife cried above the howl of the storm and the snap-and-crackle of the fire-fight. 'The inner compound!'

The inner compound?' both of her listeners gasped.

'It's the only way. Come on.' Braving the machine-gun fire, she started to run through the snow to the gate that led into the inner camp, leaving them to gape at her back and tell themselves that she was running straight into the final trap.

FIVE

A vicious burst of machine-gun fire raked the snow-filled air just in front of the running men. Schulze hardly faltered. He threw the grenade straight upwards at the tower. There was a flash of violet angry light and the shooting ceased. They ran on. A bullet slammed into the wall just above One-Flipper's head.

'The gate!' Irma cried. 'There's someone behind the gate!'

One-Flipper instinctively fired from the hip. There was

a howl of pain and the firing stopped. They ran on.

Now the gate to the inner compound loomed out of the snow in front of them. Schulze slammed his foot against it. It didn't give. One of the guards had managed to lock it before he had been shot down. To his right, Schulze saw the beam of the remaining searchlight coming towards them. Desperately, his eyes blinded by the driving snow, he sought and found the padlock. Placing his machine pistol against it and praying that there would be no failure now, he pressed the trigger. The hasp howled off into the darkness and the gate swung open in the same instant that the searchlight bathed them in its blinding light. But before the unknown machine gunner could open up, the Wotan men had tumbled through the gate and into the dead ground in a crazy rush.

Gasping and panting for air and ignoring the scarlet stab of rifle-fire, they followed the woman. 'To the prison blocks,' she cried. 'We'll release the prisoners!'

'Of course!' One-Flipper yelled in delight at the idea. 'We'll let the whole bunch run free. It'll upset the whole damn apple-cart . . . Schulze and Matz, get the men on the job . . . Open up the blocks!'

Now the Wotan started to run from hut to hut, bursting open the locks with a rapid burst of fire. Yellow lights broke the blackout everywhere. '*Get out . . . get out . . .*' the Wotan men urged. '*You're free!*'

'*FREI!*'

'*LIBRE!*'

'*VRIJ!*'

The hoarse, unbelieving cries went up on all sides in half a dozen languages. Men and women tumbled out of the huts everywhere, grabbing whatever weapons they could find, knives, shovels, picks, staves, and the slaughter commenced. First the *Kapos* and then the guards. Some were simply trampled to death, with a dozen screaming, frantic men and women, fighting each other to stamp their boots down on the hated faces of their tormentors.

Schulze, busy looting the Commandant's office of what food and drink he could find there, while Matz guarded him with his machine pistol, saw through the window how a huge man cornered one of the guards, who accepted his slaughter without a cry, knowing the futility of calling out for mercy, allowing the prisoner to saw through his throat tamely like a dumb animal.

No one paid any attention to the Wotan men now. They stuck together in close formation, weapons levelled to all sides as they backed out of the camp, heading for the waiting truck, stepping over the bodies of the slain, concentrating on keeping together in the mad howling confusion of the storm and the massacre of the guards. Then they had done it. They were out of the main gate of the outer camp, leaving behind them the last of the pyjama-striped inmates standing there in the yellow light of the sentry post, suddenly listless and drained of all emotion, as if the liberation of the camp itself had exhausted their concept of freedom; as if suddenly they realized that there was nowhere to go.

But the Wotan knew where to go. They didn't need One-Flipper to tell that by now the whole countryside would be alerted. In spite of the tremendous storm, Army units would be rushing to the scene of the great breakout from Bergedorf, Reinbek, Hamburg, ready to slaughter any inmate who dared venture out, prepared to herd them back into their miserable huts to wait for the terrible vengeance that the General SS would wreak upon them. They had to take a dive – and take it soon.

Five minutes later the packed truck had vanished into the night, heading northwards towards the bridge across the Elbe at Lauenburg . . .

SIX

The plan was a hasty improvization, flung together in the hour or so it took the truck with its shattered windscreen, and its freezing occupants, to reach the great bridge that spanned the River Elbe at Lauenburg. All three of them had worked on it, using their experience of six years of war, knowing that in a Germany which was rife with deserters and foreign slave workers, who had fled from the brutalities of their overseers, there would be no hope for them, without official travel orders, of making a successful escape from the area, which would soon be swarming with troops and police.

'Always do the unexpected, Schulze, I agree with that,' One-Flipper echoed the NCO's words, his good arm around his wife as they huddled there in the icy misery of the back of the truck. 'But what is the unexpected in our particular case, eh?' He pressed his wife, as if to encourage her not to give up hope.

'Let's put it like this, sir,' Schulze cried above the howl of the wind. 'We're not going to go much further in this truck. That shattered windscreen is a dead give-away. Besides, without a permit we're not going to get any more gas.'

'What kind of wheels do you suggest then, Schulze?' Matz asked. 'The railway?'

'Yes.'

'But to get aboard a train we'd need tickets and, above all, a travel permit – and they're checked by the chaindogs at the platform barriers, you ought to know that, Schulze?' One-Flipper objected.

'Not on troop trains,' Schulze yelled back. 'Once the chaindogs have got you on a troop train heading for the front, they couldn't care less. The cannonfodder's on the way and they can go back to the nice warm kips and their fat fraus.'

'Right indeed, wonder-boy,' Matz said scornfully. 'But how's the like of us to get on a troop train? I knew the main Berlin-Hamburg-Cologne line runs through Lauenburg, but it doesn't mean that the east-west axis train[1] will

[1] During the war for the swifter and more efficient moving of troops from one front to the other, the main railway lines were run on an east-west, south-north axis basis.

stop at that one-horse dump, does it now?'

'Exactly, my little crippled friend,' Schulze said easily, the first vague elements of a plan starting to form up in his fertile brain. 'But what if a little accident forced that east-west axis train to make an emergency stop? Do you think afterwards the train commander would go through the compartments counting bodies and discovering that he had a couple of dozen brave lads more than when he had started out?' He shook his big head. 'No, I think not.'

'Do you mean,' One-Flipper asked eagerly, 'we hold up the troop train and slip aboard in the confusion?'

'Exactly. Once we get to Cologne, we do a bunk. The Amis are only a matter of kilometres away in the Eifel now. It'd be as easy as falling off a log for you and your good lady to go over to them. But first things first, sir. Now this is how I see it . . .'

The great troop train, bearing reinforcements from the East being switched to the Western Front, started to slow down as it approached the river. Ahead of it in the dying snow-storm, the road-and-rail bridge across the Elbe came into view. As regulations prescribed, the middle-aged, grizzled driver pulled his steam whistle once, twice, three times. At ten kilometres an hour the locomotive, bearing the usual white-painted legend on its metal side '*WHEELS ROLL FOR VICTORY*', began to roll on to the long bridge, the driver, eyes narrowed against the wind and flying smoke, staring out at his side, the fireman doing the same at his.

The great metal driving wheels clattered across the trestles. The smoke flew up. Below them the Elbe stirred sluggishly, its sides already thick with ice, only an occasional barge breaking up the monotonous grey flow. Behind in the train, the dirty, ragged reinforcements packed in the fetid smoke-filled trucks and compartments snored on blindly. Hamburg, their first stop since the border, was still half an hour away. There they would receive their ersatz nigger-sweat and, if they were lucky, the Red Cross might have a hunk of black bread and a scrape of ersatz black treacle syrup to go with it. Everything was normal, routine – miserable.

The long, slow train was halfway across now. Out of the white haze of the dying storm, the first buildings of the little riverside town started to come into view and the grizzled driver thought longingly of the days on the old Hamburg-Berlin run when the buxom blonde canteen-owner's daughter at the little station to their right front had been generous, very generous, with her ample favours, especially if the man had happened to be an engine-driver with good prospects and a fine pension to look forward to. 'My God,' he told himself, mentally performing once again those bedroom gymnastics of ten years before, 'hadn't she got a pair of fine lungs on her!'

'*Lokführer!*' the fireman's urgent cry cut into his erotic memories. 'Look – '

'*Holy shit* – ' Instinctively the driver applied the brakes, forcing down the lever with all the strength his brawny arm possessed.

The big locomotive shuddered violently, strained at every rivet. Fiery sparks shot from the suddenly locked wheels. There was ear-splitting screech of metal. The fireman closed his eyes and moaned piteously, knowing now that a head-on crash was inevitable.

Metre by metre they came closer to the object blocking the line. Grimly the driver hung on. Would the brakes never bring the big train to a stop? There was a stink of overheated metal. In the carriages behind, frightened, alarmed men wakened from their heavy sleep by the howl of steel on steel. The driver started considering going over the side into the Elbe so far below. And then when it seemed that the collision could not be avoided, the locomotive came to a shuddering halt and the ashen-faced fireman felt the hot urine begin to trickle down his right leg unpleasantly. They had done it . . .

The *Haupsturmführer* with the one leg took a last look at the shattered truck suspended high in the air at the end of the mobile crane's boom, then he brought his arm down sharply. The crane-driver let go of the magnetic grip. The truck fell immediately, hurtling down to disappear into the icy waters of the Elbe, bobbed up once more, before vanshing for good in a stream of obscenely bursting air-bubbles.

'Well, what do you make of it *Hauptsturm*?' the Gestapoman in the ankle-length leather coat asked, shifting the stump of his unlit cigar from one gold molar to the other.

The one-legged soldier shrugged. 'Who knows, *Kommissar*? It might have been a plant; the bastards might have gotten away with it. It's their truck all right, that's for sure.'

'*Got away with it?*' the *Kommissar* protested. 'In this weather and with half of Schleswig-Holstein[1] looking for them – come on, *Hauptsturm*, pull the other, it's got bells on it!'

'It's no skin off'n my hooter, one way or other, *Kommissar*. Come on, let's get out of this shitting cold. It'll have the eggs off'n me!'

Together, the two of them trudged back down the track towards the station canteen, where a somewhat fading blonde was serving ersatz nigger-sweat and firewater to the sweating rescue crew. Behind them, the engine-driver, his eyes slightly glazed from the same 'medicine', started to let out the throttle. The wheels shuddered, slipping on the track, steam pouring in a white cloud from the boiler, and then with a violent jerk the train began to move forward, gathering speed at every instance.

Crowded among the snoring mass of field-grey sprawled in the lice-ridden straw of the rear boxcar, Schulze raised his bottle of schnapps to Matz in silent toast. They had done it again.

[1] The province in which Lauenburg is located.

Epilogue

In the far distance, the last of the day's barrage ended, flushing the winter sky a dull pink for a few moments to die away leaving a dull leaden-grey once more. Now there was no noise save the slow chatter of an Ami machine gun, hacking away like an irate woodpecker, which could not penetrate the bark of the tree he had chosen for his evening meal.

Carefully Schulze raised himself from the snow-filled hollow from which he had been observing the Ami hedgehogs for the last hour and pumped his right hand up and down several times: the infantry signal for advance.

Matz, who had been spotting him the whole time, bent down and gave *Frau Doktor* Flosse a hand. 'Time to go now, sir,' he said, speaking to One-Flipper, who, like his wife, was now dressed in the nondescript uniform of a private in one of the new People's Grenadier Divisions.

One-Flipper nodded and unslinging the rifle he had been carrying, dropped it in a nearby shell-crater. 'Won't be needing that any more,' he said, as if trying to reassure himself. His wife pressed his arm and together, bent double, they crept towards where Schulze waited for them, swinging his keen gaze from left to right, surveying the all-too obvious Ami positions, trying to make up his mind which was the best way for the two fugitives to get through the enemy front.

'Well, you big rogue,' One-Flipper demanded, 'what now?'

'Two o'clock, sir, shell-crater and damaged tree,' Schulze rapped, as if he were on some peacetime manoeuvre, answering an umpire's question. 'Dead ground on both sides. Easy to penetrate enemy positions, sir!'

One-Flipper laughed hollowly, a strange sound in that dead waste. 'Now don't go all military on me, Schulze. Just as I am resigning my commission and trying to make a go of it as a civilian.' He frowned abruptly. 'That is if the

Amis'll let me.'

'Of course they will, sir. You've just got to get through the front-swine. You know how the hairy-arsed stubble-hoppers are? Shoot first and ask the time of day later. Those rear-echelon stallions will lap up what you have to tell 'em like ready money. All that stuff about Goering and Himmler and the papers, etc. Why, sir,' he added with forced enthusiasm, taking in One-Flipper's trusting look and his wife's pathetic desire to believe that everything would work out well, 'ain't you got an American-Jewish mother-in-law? Who could lose with that kind of muscle on your side!'

The two of them laughed softly. One-Flipper held out his one hand, which clutched the Malacca cane, that seemed somehow incongruous, now that he wore the rough field-grey of an ordinary private, and tapped Schulze's big shoulder affectionately. 'Thanks, Sergeant-Major.'

Frau Doktor Flosse could not restrain her emotions so easily. She pressed her lips against Schulze's unshaven cheek. 'Thanks, oh my God, *thanks*! You have been so wonderful to us, *really*!'

Matz's bottom lip dropped open foolishly. Schulze was actually blushing!

'And what are you two rogues going to do now?' One-Flipper asked, busily preparing himself to lead his wife through no-man's land, sticking his greatcoat tails back, thrusting his cane into his belt, checking that he had no loose metal equipment which might clink and give their presence away to the Amis.

'Us?' Schulze said slowly. He tilted his helmet to the back of his cropped head and scratched it like some village idiot, wondering where the raindrops hitting the summer dust at his big feet might be coming from. 'I 'spect we'll soldier on, don't you, Matz?'

Matz nodded slowly. 'Yes, I should imagine that's what we'll do.'

'Soldier on,' One-Flipper echoed, obviously only half-listening now, too busy with his own immediate problems, then he took his wife's arm. 'Irma, let's go. The light is beginning to fade now.'

'Good luck to you, sir – and your wife,' Matz said.

'*Hals und Beinbruch*',[1] Schulze added, giving the officer the traditional SS parting.

'*Oh ja, Hals und Beinbruch*,' One-Flipper repeated the old phrase, as if he were hearing it for the first time. '*Danke!*'

And then they had turned and were making their way carefully, bodies half-crouched, picking their way through the shell-craters towards the Ami lines. The two old heads watched them for a while, as the growing gloom started to gather them up into its dark clutches.

'A cripple and a Yid, some start for a new life,' Schulze said softly, almost as if speaking to himself. 'A cripple and a Yid.'

'Better than nothing, Schulzi,' Matz said equally reflectively.

'I suppose you're right.'

A flare dropped from the darkening sky like a fallen angel and Schulze knew it was time to go and return to the survivors. From across the snowy fields he could already hear their hoarse voices chanting that proud Wotan marching song of the years of victory:

'SOUND THE TRUMPET,
BEAT THE DRUM,
CLEAR THE STREET,
FOR THE MEN OF WO-TAN!'

He felt the old shiver of pride and power at the thought of that long-dead formation, one thousand strong, the élite of the élite, stamping arrogantly through some newly conquered town, eyes on a distant object known only to them, confident blond giants, disdaining to look at the miserable vanquished, who regarded them like gods from another world. 'Come on, Matzi,' he cried, new hope in his

[1] Roughly 'happy landings'.

voice. 'Wotan ain't finished yet – not by a long chalk . . .' Without waiting for his old comrade, he started to stride back the way they had come, his ears full of that tremendous, bold chant:

'SOUND THE TRUMPET,
BEAT THE DRUM,
CLEAR THE STREET,
FOR THE MEN OF WO-TAN!'

'W-O-T-A-N . . .' It seemed to go on for ever . . .